TOBY

and the

MAN

A Young Boy's Personal Relationship
with Jesus, the Christ

F. Daniel McClure, PhD

ISBN 978-1-64299-058-4 (paperback)
ISBN 978-1-64299-059-1 (digital)

Christian Faith Publishing, Inc.
832 Park Avenue
Meadville, PA 16335
www.christianfaithpublishing.com

Printed in the United States of America

CONTENTS

ACKNOWLEDGMENT

S OMETIMES THE SPIRIT MOVES IN ways that are obvious to us, but most often we only see movements of the Spirit with the benefit of hindsight. When Toby was first conceived, it was never intended for publication. The inspiration for Toby was my grandson, Warner McClure, and it was simply intended to be a little story that I had hoped would introduce Warner to Jesus and perhaps be part of my legacy to him. Toby was written in a series of fits and starts over several years, and during long periods of inactivity it languished at the bottom of my sock drawer. Had I not made an offhand comment to my brother, Leonard, in a telephone conversation one evening, I'm confident that Toby would be residing among my socks to this day.

In the course of this particular conversation I happened to mention that I had been writing a children's story, and Leonard asked to see what I had done. I sent it to him, and to my surprise he not only liked what he read, but he was actually excited about it and adamant that it should be published. His enthusiasm and excitement were contagious, and ultimately became the driving force behind seeing Toby through to its completion.

Leonard and his wife Brenda were sources of immeasurable support and encouragement throughout the process. They pored through a number of drafts and provided a wealth of insightful and valuable feedback. I often drew upon their extensive biblical and theological knowledge, and on several occasions they saved me from great shame and embarrassment by spotting egregious errors I had made. As we neared the end of this process Leonard spent countless hours in painstaking editing and research to ensure that the grammar, punctuation, and the like were both correct and consistent throughout the text. His dedication and devotion to Toby have brought us to where we are today. He's my big brother and I've always held him in very high esteem. Becoming closer to him as we toiled away together on Toby has been a blessing.

I often envision our "Pop" looking down from Heaven, just scratching his head and smiling. Scratching his head at the notion that I could actually string a series of coherent sentences together, and smiling over the fact that Leonard finally got to make use of that Master's Degree in English he earned so long ago.

The Lord indeed works in strange and mysterious ways his wonders to perform.

SECTION I

Stranger in a Strange Land

CHAPTER 1

A Very Bad Day

"Blessed are those who mourn,
for they will be comforted."
Matthew 5:4

TOBY'S HAVING A BAD DAY. Since his dad died, it seems Toby's been having more bad days than good. It's been two years, but to Toby it seems like it just happened yesterday. He came home from school, just like any other day. He threw the front door open, tossed his backpack aside, kicked off his shoes, and hollered, "Mom! I'm home!" on his way to the kitchen to get a snack.

As he closed the door he suddenly stopped. Something was different. He slowly walked down the hallway, and when he passed by the living room he knew right away that something was terribly wrong. His mother was sitting in the big chair crying, and standing around her were her sister, their neighbor, and some lady he didn't know, and they were crying, too. And kneeling in front of her, whispering softly to her was their preacher from church. Toby had a terrible sinking feeling right in the pit of his stomach.

That was how Toby learned that his dad had been killed in an automobile accident. And nothing in Toby's world had been the same since. Everything had changed. They couldn't afford to keep living in their house anymore, so they moved to an apartment in a neighborhood not too far from their house, but in kind of a rough area. His mom had changed. She had to work long hours in a diner in addition to a part-time job just to make ends meet. She was no longer there when he got home from school in the afternoon. She was at work. Even though it had been two years, she was still sad; and sometimes late at night Toby would wake up and hear her crying. Despite it all, though, she took good care of Toby. She provided the things that he needed, and always spent time with him in the evenings, even though he could tell she was really tired.

Toby had changed, too. He went from being a happy-go-lucky, carefree little boy to being angry and at times spiteful—and even a little mean. He felt cheated. He felt like he didn't deserve what had happened to him. And most of all he didn't understand why this had happened to him—he hadn't done anything to give God a reason to do this. It wasn't fair. It made him mad that other children had parents who didn't die. And he especially resented other boys who still had their dads. Even though people were sympathetic toward him and tried to understand his pain, he knew there was no way they could ever know how he felt. He felt angry. Alone, confused, and misunderstood, too, but mostly just angry.

The only thing that didn't change was their church. Both his mom and dad had been active in their church and were very close to the preacher, the youth minister, and many in the congregation. Toby's mom still tried to stay involved with the church, even though she had to work so much. She was determined that this would be the one stable thing in Toby's life. So Toby still went to Sunday School and church every Sunday, even though she couldn't go with him. She also signed him up for a number of after-church activities that would keep him busy while she was working. She hoped that this would be the one constant in his otherwise topsy-turvy world. Plus, she had always found great comfort and joy through her religion and through the church. She hoped that Toby would as well.

There's just one problem: Toby hates Sundays. Just hates them. First of all, his mom has to work all day at the diner, so he has to spend his whole day at church. He has to wear a shirt and tie, which are uncomfortable, and his "good shoes" really hurt his feet. Since his mom goes to work early, he has to walk all the way to church by himself. In his good shoes, no less. And although he has the same friends at church, they seem different somehow to Toby. Plus, they have fathers. Anyway, by the time he gets to church, Toby's rarely in a good mood. And today was even worse. Today he woke up late, and it was raining. He was really hungry, but he didn't have time to eat. And worst of all, he searched all over the apartment for an umbrella, but he just couldn't find one.

Toby was a master of short-cuts. He could get just about anywhere quicker than people who went the regular way. He had discovered a short-cut to the church that took him through people's backyards, over a couple of fences, across a little creek, and then across the playground right behind the church. But today the fences were slick and hard to climb, especially in his "good shoes," and the creek was muddy. By the time he finally got to the church he was even madder than usual. He was cold and wet, his good shoes were all muddy, and his feet hurt. He almost turned back and went home, but he knew this would upset his mom, so he gritted his teeth and went in.

Which may have been a mistake as it turned out.

He got into trouble in Sunday School. His teacher was talking about the importance of a personal relationship with Jesus. Well, Toby wasn't sure he wanted a personal relationship with anyone, and besides, he never understood what that really meant. He had heard other people talking about having a personal relationship with Jesus, and he had often been told that he should have a personal relationship with Jesus. It seemed so important that he never dared to tell anyone he didn't know what the heck it meant. He just smiled and nodded whenever anyone started talking about it, and then found an excuse to get away as quick as he could.

But today he was simply in no mood to think about this stuff. It hurt his head to even try to think about it. He finally decided he was doing just fine without a personal relationship with Jesus, thank you very much. So while his teacher was talking, Toby got a pencil and just started doodling on a piece of paper. Lost in his own thoughts, he was startled when he heard his name being called out, and not in a good way. It was his Sunday School teacher. "Toby, please pay attention! This is important. Put down the pencil and listen."

Toby was embarrassed. He put the pencil down, but he didn't listen. After the lesson there was a group discussion, but since he wasn't paying attention to the lesson, Toby didn't participate. When his teacher asked that he participate, Toby refused. When the teacher insisted, Toby argued with him again, and finally muttered under his breath, "Well, my dad had a personal relationship with Jesus. If it was all that good, then why is he dead?" At that point the teacher decided that Toby would be better off sitting in the hallway until Sunday School was over.

All through church Toby fumed over how embarrassing it was to have to sit in the hall. All he could think about was how upset and disappointed his mom was going to be. The more he thought about it the more he just wanted to go home. But he couldn't. After church he had to do "mission work"; he and his friends spent Sunday afternoons going to the homes of older folks and helping them with yard work or cleaning, or running errands for them. Sometimes they would just sit with them and keep them company for a little while, and they would always give the boys lemonade or iced tea to drink. Toby liked this part the best. But not today. Today he'd had enough.

After church he just sat on a curb by the street, sitting in the rain, pouting, trying real hard not to cry. When his friends came to find him, he was still fuming. He refused to go with them. "I've had it!" he said. "Why do all that work for nothing? That's just dumb! If I'm gonna work, I'm gonna get paid! You can go ahead if you want, but I'm going home!"

His friends were shocked. "What's wrong with you, Toby? We do this every week! You know that!"

"Well, not this week we don't," muttered Toby under his breath.

"And we don't do it for money, either, Toby," they cried. "We do it for God . . . we do it for Jesus . . . it's service to others, a way of showing his love to others . . . and besides, you'll get in trouble if you don't go with us. Now, come on, hurry up and change your clothes. You're going to make us late!"

At that moment Toby realized that he had been in such a hurry this morning he had completely forgotten to bring his work clothes. Well, that was just the icing on the cake. "I don't care what you say, I'm not going!" he shouted. "If you want to do service to others," he said sarcastically, "you go right ahead, but not me . . . and you know what? I'll tell you something else. I just don't care! I don't care about service; I don't care about love, whatever that is; I don't care about God; I don't care about a personal relationship with Jesus . . . and I don't care about you."

They gasped. "Toby," they cried, "how can you say such things? What is wrong with you?"

But Toby was done. As he turned to leave he picked up the nearest stone and just gave it a fling, without any thought as to where it might land. Well, you guessed it. *Crash!* The rock went right through the front room window of Ms. Yancey—Ms. Yancey! The meanest old woman on the whole block! Toby's anger was very quickly replaced by panic. Everyone was afraid of Ms. Yancey! Some kids even said she was a witch or something! And a face-to-face with some mean old witch was the last thing Toby needed on a morning like this! He turned and just started running full blast through the rain. He passed the back of the church and rounded the corner, cutting across the neighborhood playground. He kept his head down against the rain, just staring at the ground, while his little legs churned just as fast as they possibly could. All he could think about was getting home as soon as possible.

That's why he didn't see that metal post. You know, the big one, the one that holds up the basketball net. *Wham!* He hit it at full speed. He felt sick. When he was able to open his eyes a little he actually did see the post. It was looming way above him. He was flat on his back, looking straight up at it. And it was spinning around in circles. In fact, the whole world was spinning around. It made Toby dizzy. He thought maybe if he closed his eyes it would all stop. And that's when everything went black.

CHAPTER 2

Are You Famous?

"I will send my messenger ahead of you, who will prepare your way, a voice of one calling in the wilderness, 'Prepare the way for the Lord, make straight paths for him.'"

Mark 1:2-3

WHEN TOBY AWOKE HE WAS still lying on his back, looking up. It was daylight and boy was it bright. Maybe the brightest daylight he'd ever seen. He was afraid. He closed his eyes, and then it came to him. *People who have those near-death experiences always talk about seeing incredibly bright light, the brightest light ever,* he thought. Then it hit him! "Oh, no!" he cried out, "I'm dead!" He looked around in the brightness and saw nothing. He was alone. Then he looked down. His Sunday School clothes were gone. Instead, he was wearing some kind of linen robe. Instead of underwear he had on sort of a loincloth, like he tried to do with a towel one time when he was pretending to be Tarzan. His good shoes were also gone, and on his feet were some kind of sandals.

Oh, now I get it, Toby said to himself as if he had solved a great mystery. *I'm not dead. I'm in the hospital. This big robe is a really a hospital gown.* But he didn't feel bad, so why would he need to be in a hospital? In fact, he felt pretty good. Better than he'd felt in a long time, for some reason. He finally laid back, feeling very relaxed, and just rested very comfortably against a little hill of sand and rock.

He sat straight up with a start. *Hey, wait a minute! Sand and rock?????? Hospitals have beds, not sand and rocks!* he thought. Now he was really confused. The more he looked around the more he realized—this wasn't a hospital at all! And as he looked around some more, he realized it wasn't even his home town! His home town had trees and houses and sidewalks. But this place had none of that. In fact, it looked just like a desert. Flat land, sand and rocks, and no grass, just scrub bushes and a few short, stubby trees. And boy was it hot!

Hot!?!? Then it hit him. The only place that Toby had ever heard of that matched this description was . . . well, you-know-where . . . where bad people end up after they die.

Oh No! Toby thought. *No! . . . No! . . . I take it all back. I didn't mean all those things I said . . . I was just mad . . . please listen, just give me another chance!* He began to cry.

He suddenly looked up, and in the distance he saw someone walking toward him. A man. And this man was wearing a linen tunic a lot like the one Toby had on. Toby felt strange all of a sudden. He thought he should probably be afraid, but for some reason he wasn't. He couldn't explain it. As the man drew near, Toby got a good look at his face, and he didn't know how or why, but he instantly knew he wasn't in you-know-where.

Toby never gave much thought as to whether people looked kind or not. And he didn't know what made him notice, but this man had the kindest face Toby had ever seen. His hair was down to his shoulders and he wore a full beard, and the hood of his tunic was pulled over his head to protect him from the sun and the blowing desert sand. But somehow Toby could still tell how kind he was. He figured it must have been the man's eyes.

As the man drew close he looked down and very matter-of-factly said, "Hello Toby." Just like that.

Well, Toby was beside himself with wonder. "Hey, how do you know my name? Do I know you?" he asked. "Who are you? Where am I? Where are we? What am I doing here?"

But the man just kept walking. After he had gone a ways he casually looked over his shoulder and simply said, "Follow me."

Toby scrambled to his feet and ran after the man. He had a thousand questions running through his head, but before he could say a word, the man stopped, knelt down, placed his hands on Toby's shoulders, and looked him right in the eye.

"Don't say anything, Toby," the man said very quietly, "just listen." All of a sudden Toby felt calm. He relaxed and did exactly as he was told. "Toby, I'm about to go on a very important mission, and I'm going to need your help. For right now, though, your job is to just watch and observe. Don't talk. Don't say anything—just do as I say." Toby gulped and tried to speak, but the words just wouldn't come. He closed his eyes, and the best he could do was just a slight nod of his head.

They went on walking. After a little while they crossed over a little sand hill and Toby saw a sight that almost took his breath away. Below them was a beautiful valley, with a river running through the middle of it, and there was a large crowd of people gathered around on the near side of the river.

Right in the middle of the river was this "wild man." Instead of a tunic like Toby and his friend, this man covered himself with animal skins. Toby heard the man excitedly shouting to the crowd, "Repent! Repent!" Toby wasn't exactly sure what this meant, but he knew it must be important because of the way the man was shouting it. And the next thing you know, people start wading into the river over to this man, and he's dunking them in the river, one right after the other!

Just as Toby was about to ask what in the world was going on, his friend turned to him and, holding Toby's face in his hand, said, "Stay right here. Don't move from this spot. I have something important to take care of. That's the Jordan River down there, and that man is named John, they call him John the Baptist. He's baptizing people down there in the river, and I'm going to ask him to baptize me, too. In the meantime, I want you to stay here and wait." Toby nodded. Something about what the man said sounded very familiar, but Toby just couldn't put his finger on it. He heard a man in the crowd shout out to the wild man, "Are you the messiah?" But John didn't even look up. He just kept right on baptizing and loudly said, "I baptize you with water. But one who is more powerful than I will come, the straps of whose sandals I am not worthy to untie. He will baptize you with the Holy Spirit and fire."

As Toby pondered these and other strange happenings, the man continued walking down the hill. When he reached the bottom of the hill he turned and without hesitation just walked right into the river! As he waded into the water toward the wild man, Toby watched as the crowd parted to let him through. He walked right up to the man and the two of them faced each other. Toby all of a sudden felt a shiver go up his spine, but he didn't know why. There was one thing he did know, though. Something was up. Something was afoot. Something big.

While the two men faced each other, they started to speak, but Toby couldn't hear what was being said. Then the wild man knelt down in the river, like he wanted Toby's friend to baptize him. But his friend said something and the wild man stood, turned his face to the heavens like he was saying a prayer, and then dunked his friend right into the river, just like he had done with all the others. But when the man lifted his friend out of the water, strange things started to happen. First of all, the clouds above the river parted in two, and the brightest light Toby had ever seen shone down on his friend. Then he heard this voice, this loud booming voice. He looked around to see who was talking, but he didn't see anyone—it was coming out of the sky! And the voice said, "This is my son in whom I am well pleased."

At that very moment a bird flew out of the space between the clouds, a little white dove. And that little dove came down and rested right on his friend's shoulder! Toby was amazed. The dove flew off into the sky, and his friend turned and started walking out of the river. But he was going the wrong way! He was heading away from Toby, toward the mountainous desert.

Just as Toby was beginning to fear that he had been forgotten, the man turned his head ever so slightly, looked right at Toby, and gave a little nod. Toby got the message! He scrambled off that hill and ran as fast as his feet would carry him down the hill and toward his friend. This time he kept his head up though. He was very careful to look where he was going.

When he reached his friend's side he was breathless, but not breathless enough to keep him from shouting, "Awesome . . . that was amazing! That was incredible! I've never seen anything like it! What was that all about, anyway? And by the way, who are you? . . . Are you famous or something?"

His friend smiled and glanced down at Toby. He gave Toby a little wink, and with a chuckle he quietly said, "Not yet, Toby. Not yet."

And he kept on walking.

A Run-In With Evil

"At once the Spirit sent him out into the wilderness, and he was in the wilderness forty days, being tempted by Satan. He was with the wild animals, and angels attended him."

Mark 1:12-13

THE NEXT THING TOBY KNEW, they were walking into a wilderness, a wild, barren place with lots of high mountains. It felt strange, and seemed a little spooky to Toby. He started to feel a little afraid, but he didn't say anything. He just kept walking. When they got close to the highest mountain his friend stopped. Again he knelt, placed his hands on Toby's shoulders, looked him in the eye, and said: "This isn't going to be easy, Toby. There's someone up there, someone who has been my arch enemy since the beginning of time. And I'm going to have to face him. There are some things that I'm going to have to settle with him once and for all."

"Why?" asked Toby.

"Well," his friend said, "he wants to keep me from my mission. You see, I have been given certain powers, but these powers have a special purpose. A very special purpose. And he wants to keep me from using these powers to do what I need to do. He believes that if he can tempt me to do certain things with these powers he'll keep me from my mission. And if he is able to do that, he'll win. He's a pretty desperate character right now, so he's going to try everything he can to defeat me."

Now Toby was really afraid. He began to speak, but his friend cut him off, saying, "I can tell that you're a little frightened. And you should know that things may get a little strange up there. We'll be up there for a while, for about forty days. And while we're up there I'm not going to eat anything. We call that fasting. And I'll be fasting and praying until we're done."

This worried Toby a little bit. Fasting? No food? Forty days? He had only been there a little while, and he was already hungry. He knew he couldn't make it for forty days! At home he could barely make it to dinner time without a snack. But his friend sensed his discomfort. He shook his head, smiling, and said, "And you'll have plenty of food and water, so don't worry, you'll be fine. You won't be fasting. You won't go hungry. You'll have plenty to eat. But this is important—no matter what happens, don't offer any to me. Under any circumstances. Do not tempt me."

Toby gulped and nodded. After a brief pause his friend added, "And you may see and hear some pretty strange things up there. My enemy can be quite a scary sight, and he's mean. Really mean. But you don't have to be afraid. You will be protected. You'll be safe, no matter what. You'll just have to trust me on that." Then he seemed to relax a little bit, and he smiled at Toby and said, "Now, this is going to keep me busy, and it's going to take all of my strength and all of my attention." After a pause, he added, "And a lot of faith, too, a whole lot of faith."

He went on, "So I won't have a lot of time for you during this ordeal. All of my energy will be devoted to the struggle . . . now, I know how inquisitive you are, and I know you're going to have a million questions. But you'll just have to hold them and keep them to yourself for a while. There'll be plenty of time for us to talk after this is over."

And off they went.

Boy, was his friend ever right. It was really scary. Even though it was the middle of the day when they reached the top of the mountain, all of a sudden things got kind of dark, like it gets just before twilight. And cold, too, for some reason. His friend made a place behind a mound of rocks where Toby could safely hide. Toby settled in, and his friend left. Before long Toby began to hear the sounds of a terrible struggle going on. He peeked around the corner once, but was so frightened by what he saw that he never peeked again. But he heard the goings on. He heard the struggle.

He heard a voice, a horrible, terrible voice. He decided that anyone with a voice like that had to be bad, very bad. Then it dawned on him—this must be the enemy his friend had mentioned. To Toby he was the "Bad Man"! He heard this Bad Man heap all kinds of abuse on his friend. It was obvious that his friend was fasting and that he was very hungry and a little weak. So the Bad Man began to mock him, saying bad things about his father. He said things like, "Hah! Where's your father now? Look at you! What kind of father lets his own son go hungry like this?" And then he dared him to use his powers to turn the stones on the ground into bread. That way he could eat; he wouldn't go hungry. And there were so many stones on the ground! He'd be able to feed all his friends, too. Well, Toby thought that sounded like a pretty good deal. But just as he was beginning to really enjoy the idea of eating a little something, he heard his friend refuse. He turned and faced the Bad Man and in a very strong voice he said, "Man cannot live by bread alone, but by every word that comes from God."

Toby wasn't sure what that meant, but it sounded like his friend was saying that there are more important things in our lives than just not being hungry. But Toby was still really hungry. His stomach was growling. He was still pretty sure he'd have gone for the food.

Then, out of nowhere, Toby felt a huge *whoosh!* of wind. Things felt like they were moving really fast. And then all of a sudden it felt like they were in a whole different place. He peeked around the rocks and saw that he was right! They were sitting on top of a huge building, looking down on a beautiful city, way below. He heard the Bad Man say that they were on top of the Temple, the holiest place there was, and the city down below was Jerusalem. The Temple loomed majestically over the city. Suddenly things got quiet. Toby heard a very low sound, almost like an animal's growl. But it wasn't an animal—it was the Bad Man. And the Bad Man was making fun of Toby's friend. He taunted him and dared him to jump off the building. He dared him to jump off and use his powers to save himself to prove that he was someone special.

Toby thought, *Boy, I'd show him all right! I'd jump right off this building and come back and just laugh in his face. That's what I'd do!* But his friend didn't do that. He resisted the temptation. The more Toby thought about it, though, the more he decided his friend was probably right. In his short little life he had already learned (the hard way) not to take a dare.

Toby heard his friend say, "Do not put the Lord your God to the test."

Another *whoosh!* This time Toby understood. They were somewhere else. He was beginning to get the hang of this. He climbed up over the top of the rocks and saw that they were atop a huge mountain. And when he looked down he could hardly believe his eyes. Below them were all the kingdoms of the world! Toby had never seen anything like it before in his whole life! They were beautiful. Gleaming in the sun, full of riches, gold, silver, and all manner of wonderful things. Toby was in awe. He ducked back behind some rocks as he heard the Bad Man start talking again. This time, though, the Bad Man sounded strangely nice. He said that his friend could have them all. He would just give them to him. All of them! Just like that! And all his friend had to do was to agree that that the kingdoms were the Bad Man's to give.

Now, this is not a bad deal, Toby thought. *All the kingdoms of the world, the whole world! And all you have to do is admit that they are his to give? Hah! Piece of cake!* He was lost in his dreams of the fun that he and his friend would have with all these kingdoms, when, once again, he heard his friend refuse. But his friend didn't just refuse. He said, "It is written: 'Worship the Lord your God and serve him only!'" And then Toby heard him shout, in a loud, booming voice, "Away from me, Satan!" Toby was stunned. *Wait a minute,* he thought. *Satan?* As that thought sunk in, Toby began to understand just how bad this Bad Man was.

It seemed like this struggle had gone on forever. But then, just as quickly as it began, the ordeal came to an end. The twilight lifted and it was like regular daylight again. Toby could tell that the Bad

Man had gone because things just seemed to feel better, like a real scary storm had passed and now it was calm again. And it wasn't so cold anymore.

Toby also realized he wasn't scared anymore. He didn't realize how frightened he had been until it was over. But now he felt safe. He excitedly scurried out of his hiding place and went looking for his friend.

Just as he rounded a corner on the trail he saw his friend in the shadows over in the distance. He started to run over to him, but then quickly stopped. He was stunned at how tired and worn his friend looked, and there was this huge person with him!—this huge person, hovering over him, wiping his brow and giving him food and water. It looked like maybe a doctor or someone tending to him.

Except this guy was huge, and he didn't look like anyone Toby had ever seen before. He turned around and Toby stopped in his tracks. The man was not only huge, he was fearsome looking. Toby just stood there, his mouth hanging open, glued to the spot. But then the man quietly and in a very kind voice said, "Fear not, for I have come in peace." For some reason, this was very reassuring. Toby immediately felt better. And then the man just disappeared. Just like that! Poof! Gone!

Toby was amazed. He ran over and sat next to his friend, who was looking much better now.

Breathless, Toby said, "I thought it was just us! I thought we were alone up here, just you and me!" He looked bewildered. "But I saw this huge guy with you. And what a face! I've never seen anybody like him! Who in the world was that?"

"That," his friend said very matter-of-factly, "was an angel. More correctly, he's an archangel. He was sent here to minister to me, to give me comfort after my ordeal."

"What are you talking about?" Toby said. "You're pulling my leg! Come on, even I know there's no such thing as angels." He gathered up his nerve and added, "Look, I may be young, but there are some things I know, and that's one of them."

His friend gave him a look, and Toby figured there was probably nothing to be gained by arguing about this issue. So he quickly changed the subject, saying, "Well I'm glad you made it through. I'm glad you're not hurt." Then he stopped and looked his friend right in the eye, and said, "Okay, now it's over. You can tell me. What's the story? What was this 'ordeal' all about anyway?"

His friend looked off into the distance, took a deep breath, and seemed to be listening to something very far away that Toby couldn't hear. Then he turned to Toby and quietly said, "He was trying to keep me from my mission."

Toby looked up at him and said, "Yeah, yeah, the mission. I already knew that. You've mentioned this mission a couple of times, but you never really said what it is. What's this mission all about, anyway?"

His friend paused, took a deep breath, closed his eyes, and quietly said, "Toby, sometimes people don't behave the way my Father would have them behave. Sometimes they're selfish, and they use their gifts for their own selfish interests rather than helping others. Sometimes they're greedy, and they use their gifts just to get more and more things instead of helping those who don't have much. And sometimes they place their love of the things of this world above their love for my Father. Their motives are selfish and sinful. So my Father sent me here to help free people from those urges and their sinfulness so they'll behave the way He has always wanted them to. The most important thing, though, is that my mission is to do my Father's will."

Toby looked away and was quiet for a very long time. Finally, he turned his head and sadly looked down at the ground.

After a long pause he quietly said, "My father is in heaven; he was killed in a car crash."

His friend looked at him as though his heart was breaking. He quietly whispered, "I know, Toby, I know." He put his arm around Toby and after a long silence said, "But you know what? You have another Father, a Father who is also in heaven. And He's my Father, too."

Toby was shocked. "Wait a minute! What are you talking about? . . . You can only have one dad."

"That's true," his friend said, "but you also have a Heavenly Father. My Father. God."

Well, poor Toby was speechless. He felt like he had just run into that pole again. He felt dizzy, like the whole world was spinning around again. He finally took a deep breath, and then his eyes got real wide and he said, "But if your Father is God, then that means that you're . . . you're . . . why you're Jesus!"

A kind smile lit up his friend's face. He looked at Toby and said, "You're right, Toby, I am Jesus. I'm Jesus of Nazareth. And my Father is God the Father Almighty. Just like you, though, I had a dad here on earth. His name was Joseph. He's in heaven, too, just like your dad. But God is my Father. He's my Heavenly Father . . . and He's your Heavenly Father, too."

Toby got very serious. At first he just sat there, lost in thought. But then he stood and began pacing around. His brow was furrowed, like he was doing math in his head or something. Then he stopped, and suddenly he began to beam. He excitedly ran back to Jesus. He stopped, looked up at Jesus' face, and cried, "Well, if God is your Father and God is my Father, do you know what that means?"

"Tell me," said Jesus.

Toby put his hands on his hips, threw his head back, and shouted, "It means we're kind of like brothers, Jesus! We're brothers!"

Jesus let go a laugh from way down deep inside of him. He smiled and patted Toby softly on the back and said, "Toby, my little friend, I do believe you're beginning to get the picture."

CHAPTER 4

The Twelve

"As Jesus went on from there, he
saw a man named Matthew sitting at the tax collector's booth.
'Follow me,' he told him, and Matthew
got up and followed him."

Matthew 9:9

ONE DAY TOBY WAS WALKING with Jesus on a road alongside the Sea of Galilee. There were lots of fishermen in boats along the shore. Jesus told Toby to go and sit by a rock wall across the road and wait. Toby found a nice fig tree that gave him lots of shade and watched as Jesus strolled by one of the fishing boats resting on the shore. There were two fishermen in a boat mending their nets, working so busily that they barely looked up when Jesus came near.

Then the strangest thing happened. Jesus passed by the boat and barely stopped walking. It looked like he said something to the two men. Toby thought that he must have said something import-ant, because they immediately dropped what they were doing and followed him as he moved to the shade of a nearby tree. On the way Jesus called out to two other men who were out fishing with their father. He must have said something important to them, too, because they stopped fishing and rowed their boat to the shore. The two men left their father and joined Jesus and the other two.

One of the men turned and left. He returned a little later with two other men. One of them looked like he could have been the man's brother, and they joined Jesus and the others. After a while two other men approached Jesus. Toby heard them say that they had been followers of John, that "wild man" over in the Jordan River. They said that one day when Jesus walked by them, John whispered, "Behold! The Lamb of God." They took this as a sign and set out to follow Jesus.

The following day they passed through a gate where they had to pay taxes. After they had passed through the gate, the man who was collecting the taxes just stopped what he was doing, walked away from the gate, and joined them. Later another man joined, but Toby wasn't sure where he had come from. All in all, there were twelve men who had joined Jesus.

One particular evening the group paused by the side of the road to eat and take shelter for the night. After they had eaten Jesus made a place for Toby nestled into an outcropping of rocks. Toby understood that he was to wait there until he was called. He watched as Jesus talked to the twelve men for a while. Then Jesus went off to pray, and the men talked among themselves.

Toby noticed that one man seemed to be sort of apart from the larger group. It was the man who was collecting the taxes. He always seemed to be kind of outside of the group, and every now and then he seemed to just wander aimlessly away from the rest. He wandered over in Toby's direction. He spotted Toby and came over to speak to him. The man said he had seen Toby earlier, but had not been formally introduced yet. He extended an arm in greeting, as was their custom, and said, "My name is Matthew, young man, and who might you be?" Toby stood upright and tried to be as grown up as he could be. He extended his arm to meet Matthew's and said, "Toby. My name is Toby." Matthew smiled and said, "Well, Toby, it's nice to make your acquaintance." Before he knew it, Toby heard himself saying, "Hey, how come you don't seem to fit in with the others?"

Toby realized what he had said and then quickly added, "I only said that because a lot of times I'm not part of the group, either. But with me, it's usually because they don't like me." As Toby heard these words tumble out of his mouth he was crushed. He had completely forgotten about the rule about kids speaking only when spoken to. On top of that, he had embarrassed himself and had probably been rude to this man as well. He started to apologize, but Matthew stopped him, saying, "Well, Toby, these men aren't too sure they like me, either. You see, I'm a tax collector. That is, I *was* a tax collector."

Toby said, "So what? That's not so bad is it? I mean it's just a job. Somebody has to collect the taxes, right?"

"You're right, Toby," Matthew said. "But you see, the taxes that are collected from the Jews go to the Romans." Toby still didn't seem to get the picture, so Matthew went on. "I'm a Jew, like Jesus and the rest. This is my country. But the Romans invaded and took over my country, and now they rule over us. They can be mean and cruel, and the taxes on my countrymen are very high. So they see me as kind of a traitor, taking their hard-earned money and giving it over to the Romans."

"Then why did you do it?" Toby asked. Matthew said, "Well, I guess because they paid me a lot of money. It sounds terrible when I hear myself say that, but it's the truth." He paused and looked sad. He sighed and added, "I guess I was just selfish. I didn't really think about the pain my countrymen were in so long as the Romans paid me a lot of money."

"I guess that was pretty rotten after all," Toby said before even realizing it. But Matthew seemed lost in thought. Toby hoped that Matthew had been too preoccupied with whatever he was thinking about to hear what he had just said. No such luck, though. "You're right," whispered Matthew, shaking his head. "And it's probably going to take some work for these men to forgive me."

"But here you are with them," said Toby. "That means that Jesus thought you were okay, right?" Matthew brightened a bit. "Yes, I suppose he did, as a matter of fact," he said. "In addition to being a tax collector, I was also a terrible sinner. Jesus knew very well what kind of life I had led, and he picked me anyway. I believe that he must have seen something in me that no one else had ever seen, myself included. I must have sensed something in him, too, because when he walked by all he said was 'Follow me' and I just dropped everything, left my station, left my job, left everything I owned, and followed him. That's all it took. And so here I am."

"Wait a minute," cried Toby. "Can you say that again, that thing about how he picked you?" Matthew smiled and said, "Sure I can. I was at my gate collecting taxes when Jesus came through. At first he just looked at me. And the way he looked at me, I felt like he could see right into my heart. And then he just said, 'Follow me.' And that was it. I did."

Before Toby could react, he heard a very deep voice right behind him say, "Me, too."

And then another voice said, "And I as well."

Toby was petrified. He spun around, still in shock. A very large, gruff looking man stepped out of the shadows. "Hello, Toby," the deep voice said. "My name is Simon Peter." Toby nodded, speechless. Peter continued, "And this is my brother, Andrew." Toby blurted out, "The fishermen!"

"Yes, we're hard-working fishermen. Simple men. But Jesus must have seen something good in us, too, because when he passed by us he said, 'Follow me, and I'll make you fishers of men.' He selected us to be his Disciples."

All of a sudden Toby turned around, grabbed Matthew, and began to jump up and down. He excitedly shouted, "He said the same thing to me, Matthew! He said the same thing to me!" He turned toward Peter and Andrew. "He said the same thing to me! He looked at me. He looked me right in the eye and said, 'Follow me!' And that was it! I did! That means I'm a Disciple too, right?" He whirled around and said, "He must have seen something in me too, right? He saw something in me that no one else has ever seen! He saw something good in me! He said, 'Follow me.'" Toby threw his head back and shouted at the top of his lungs, "He said the same thing to me!"

The other men gathered around to see what the commotion was all about. After Toby calmed down a little, Peter took him by the arm. Looking around, Peter said, "Well, my little friend, since you're a Disciple, too, I suppose I should introduce you to the rest." Toby beamed. Peter said, "This is James. They call him 'James the Elder' because there is another Disciple named James who is a lot younger." James nodded to Toby, and Peter said, "And this is his brother John.

They're also fishermen." Peter paused, then added, "They're the sons of Zebedee, the man you saw them fishing with. But Jesus calls them the 'Sons of Thunder' because of their strength and their devotion to him."

Peter went on: "The older gentleman next to John is Simon. We call him Simon the Zealot because he can be very excitable."

Another man stepped forward and said, "My name is Philip, and this man's name is Nathaniel." Toby looked up at the rest of the men who had gathered around him.

Peter said, "This is Thomas, and beside him stands Jude. The young boy beside Jude, he is called James, or James the Lesser, or James the Younger. He's the other James." The young man stepped forward quickly and said, "James the Just, if you don't mind, and I'm very pleased to meet you, Toby."

Peter said, "So that's it. We're Jesus' Disciples." Just then Andrew quietly tapped Peter on the shoulder. He pointed over in the shadows and whispered something in Peter's ear. Toby looked over and saw a figure standing back in the shadows by a grove of olive trees. "Oh, yes, I forgot," Peter whispered. "That man over there is the last Disciple to be chosen by Jesus. His name is Judas. Judas Iscariot. He's new, and he's not from Galilee like most of us, so we don't know much about him yet." The lone figure by the olive grove said nothing. He simply moved through the shadows as the other men made their way back over to where Jesus was waiting for them.

CHAPTER 5

Jerusalem and the Making of a Friend

"He went to the house of Mary the mother
of John, also called Mark, where many people had gathered and were praying."
Acts 12:12

TOBY LIKED IT WHEN THEY went to Jerusalem. They had been traveling up in Galilee and Perea, where there were just small towns separated either by farmland or desert. But Jerusalem was different. It was large, noisy, and filled with all kinds of people. Not just shepherds, farmers, and fishermen, like up in Galilee, but people from all over the world.

And the Temple! Toby had never seen anything so grand in his entire life. It was huge! And it had courtyards that entered into smaller courtyards, and it kept going like that until you got to a little room called the Holy of Holies. Only the High Priest of the Temple was allowed in there. The Court of the Gentiles was the largest by far, and was an area where anybody could be, even women and Gentiles, or people who weren't Jewish. Only Jews could enter the next court-yard, and then only Jewish men could enter the rest. Toby sat in the shade of a gnarled old olive tree while Jesus was teaching in an area called Solomon's Porch. It was Jesus' favorite place to teach, and the crowds that gathered to hear him kept on growing and growing. People seemed really hungry for his message.

But there were other people in the crowd who were not there because they were hungry for Jesus' message. They were there to spy on him and report back to their masters, the Jewish elders and Temple Priests. The larger the crowds got, the more worried the Jewish elders became. They were afraid of Jesus, afraid of his message, and afraid of the power he would have as more and more people flocked to him. Most of all, they were afraid that if Jesus' followers started causing trouble, they would lose their special position with their Roman occupiers. But the Romans also had spies in the crowd. They reported back to the Roman governor, Pontius Pilate, who was always on the lookout for trouble-makers who might make his life more difficult.

When Jesus had finished teaching, he called Toby over to him and said, "I want you to come with me over to a friend's house. I have to take care of some things while we're here in Jerusalem, and I want you to stay with my friends until I'm done." Toby nodded. Then Jesus said, "When I'm finished I'll come and get you and we'll join the others up on the Mount of Olives."

The pair made their way through the city and over to the house of a woman named Mary. For some reason there were tons of people in and around Jerusalem named Mary. The husband of this particular Mary had died some time ago, so she was called "the Widow Mary" to set her apart from the others. The upper room of her home had become sort of a meeting place for Jesus' followers. Peter was related to the Widow Mary in some way, perhaps cousins, and he often used the upper room of her house as a place where he would teach and spread Jesus' message to others when he was in Jerusalem.

"You'll like the Widow Mary," said Jesus. "She's very kind, and she likes children. In fact, she has a son not much older than you. His name is John Mark, but many simply call him Mark."

"Great!" said Toby, smiling. "It will be nice to be with someone close to my own age for a change."

Soon the road began to rise, and as they rounded a bend Toby looked up the hill and saw a large house surrounded by a stone wall. "That's her house up atop the hill," said Jesus. They passed through the gate and into the yard, and suddenly Jesus stopped, a smile lighting up his face. Over in the corner of the yard was a small grove of very large olive trees. In the shade of the trees a woman sat in a chair, sewing. Jesus, obviously pleased to see her, turned and said, "Toby, there's someone I'd like for you to meet. She's a very dear friend of mine, and she's a helper, too, just like you. Come." Toby hoped this wouldn't take long, because he was really hungry.

When the woman saw Jesus, she smiled and stood up and gave him a big hug. "Toby," Jesus said, "this is my good friend Mary. We call her Mary Magdalene, or Mary of Magdala, because that's the town she is from." He then turned to Mary and said, "Mary, this is my good friend and helper, Toby." Toby was thrilled to be introduced as Jesus' helper, although he didn't feel like he'd been much of a help at all.

He gave a little bow and said, "I'm very pleased to meet you, Miss Mary." She smiled at Toby, and he realized that she was beautiful. There was something about her that looked familiar, as if he had seen her before. Then he realized what it was. Whether it was the smile itself or the warmth and kindness he saw behind it, there was something in her smile that reminded him of someone, someone he loved very much.

"I'm pleased to make your acquaintance as well, Master Toby," she said. "And you must be quite a young man, because Jesus is very careful in choosing those who are to be his helpers." Toby beamed with pride, but he didn't know what to say. He was in luck, though, because before he could say anything Mary said, "Enough talk. Get on in the house, lunch is waiting, and I know you must be starved." Toby liked her even more after that.

As they neared the house a young boy came flying out of the front door and threw himself into Jesus' arms. "Jesus!" he cried, "Welcome! It's so good to see you again!"

Jesus smiled and tousled the boy's hair, and then gently set him down and said, "John Mark, I have someone I'd like you to meet." But before he could say anything else, John Mark turned to Toby excitedly and said, "Hi, I'm John Mark. Come on in, lunch is waiting!" and off they ran. Toby followed John Mark to the rear of the house and into the kitchen area. John Mark introduced Toby to his mother, who had a plate of breads and fruit for them. They each had seconds.

After lunch Toby followed John Mark as he scrambled up fifteen narrow stone steps and into a very large, open room with a long, low table right in the middle of it. John Mark said, "When my Uncle Peter is in Jerusalem he stays with us here. This room is where the men gather to eat and talk, and where my Uncle Peter teaches them and tells them about his travels with Jesus."

Toby didn't know this. He had been with the men when Jesus would send Peter to Jerusalem on various errands, but he wasn't sure where he stayed. So now he knew; Peter stayed at the home of his cousin, this Widow Mary.

"Does Peter come here often?" Toby asked.

"Not as often as I'd like," said John Mark, "but he comes whenever he can. I serve them their meals up here and then clean up when they're done. And if I'm quiet and stealthy enough, I can stay up here while they eat and I can hear what they're saying."

Toby frowned and said, "Well that's not very nice of you."

John Mark pretended to be offended. "I have my reasons," he said with a wink. John Mark went on, "After he meets with the men he sits with me and talks. He tells me about his travels with Jesus, and all about Jesus' teachings and the miracles he performs. I ask him lots of questions and get him to explain things I don't understand, because I have a plan. I've been going to school in the Temple and learning to write, and I think that someday I might just write down these stories about Jesus' sayings and teachings and miracles . . . that's why I try to stay in the room and listen to the men talk."

Toby promised John Mark that he would be among the first to read those stories. "It'll probably never happen," said John Mark, "but it's fun to think about, anyway."

John Mark continued showing Toby around the upper room. Against one wall were stacks of blankets and a number of baskets filled with linen clothing. "Those mats are for when people stay here," said John Mark, "which seems to be more and more these days. And those linens are there for anyone to wear while my mother and her friends from next door wash their garments. And from the looks of your tunic," he chided, "you'll be needing those linens very soon indeed."

Toby looked down on his filthy tunic and was a bit embarrassed, but he knew John Mark's comments were all in good fun.

At the far end of the room was a little chamber with a cot, a nightstand with a basin on it, and a number of pillows and mats all around. "This is where I sleep," said John Mark. "That is, most of the time." He then led Toby outside to a little terrace that stood about seven feet above the ground. There was no roof and no railing, just a little ledge around the rim of it. Up against the house was a stack of blankets and a few mats, and a rope that John Mark had made by tying several linens together.

He noticed Toby eying the rope and said, "That's so I can get on and off the terrace without having to go through the house and bother people." He quickly added, "This is actually my favorite place to sleep, out here where you can see the stars and hear the sounds of the night. It's very peaceful out here, and if it gets too cold, I have many blankets to keep me warm. From up here you can see lots of things. There is a wall that goes all around the city, and it has gates to get in and out. Just over there is the gate that travelers pass through from the south on their way to Jerusalem. Straight ahead is Herod's palace, and right below us, at the bottom of this hill, is the palace of Caiaphas, High Priest of the Temple. Across the way there is the Mount of Olives, or Mount Olivet, stretching over almost the entire eastern side of Jerusalem. You can't quite see the Temple from here, but during the High Holidays at night you can see the light from the torches as they perform their rituals. Next year I'll be of age and able to go," he said excitedly. Then in a much quieter voice he said, "And on a clear day you can see all the way past the city to that hill way over there." Then his voice became almost a whisper. "That hill is called Golgotha," he said. "It's where the Romans crucify criminals."

Before Toby could ask about crucifixion, John Mark led him to the corner of the terrace and said, "See this road that runs by the side of the house?" Toby craned his neck and looked around the corner of the house and nodded. "If you go straight on this road," John Mark said, "you will leave the city of Jerusalem." He pointed to the Jerusalem Gate and said, "But the road forks off to the left just before you get to the city gate, and it runs right past that horrible Golgotha and far beyond. And just before you round the bend that goes to Golgotha is the home of Joseph of Arimathea. He's a very wealthy man. He's also a Pharisee, a member of the Sanhedrin, the ruling council. The Pharisees hate Jesus . . . but Joseph doesn't. In fact, I believe that he and Jesus have secretly become friends."

"Well, if it's secret," said Toby, "how come you know about it?" John Mark ignored Toby's question and continued. "And I'd be willing to bet that his pal Nicodemus is a secret follower of Jesus as well. Jesus visits them often when he's in Jerusalem. In fact, I'll bet that's where he went today."

"Wait a minute. How do you know all this stuff?" asked Toby, a bit suspicious. "If these men are really secret followers of Jesus, how come it's not a secret to you?" John Mark looked a bit uncomfortable, like he was searching for a believable explanation. He obviously failed, because he silently motioned for Toby to follow him back into his chamber.

John Mark sat on the cot and motioned to Toby to sit next to him. He looked around to make sure no one was in the upper room with them. When he was certain that he wouldn't be overheard, he said in a low whisper, "Toby, can you keep a secret?" Toby wasn't surprised at this, because he knew something was up. He said, "Why, of course I can. What is it?"

"Well," John Mark began, "don't tell anyone, but there are lots of times that I sneak off the terrace and go to different places where I know something is happening." He looked around the room again, just to be sure no one was there, then said, "One night Jesus was here and after dark he left the house and walked up the road toward the house of Joseph of Arimathea. I was curious, so I climbed down the rope and followed him all the way to Joseph's house. Joseph met him at the door, and he went in. He stayed in there for a long time, because I had to come back here before he left, or else my mom would have known that I was missing."

Toby nodded knowingly and said, "I knew that rope was for more than just not going through the house to get outside."

John Mark smiled. "Pretty crafty, huh?"

Toby had to give it to him. It really was pretty crafty. "But wait," said Toby. "What about this Nicodemus?"

"Well," said John Mark, "one time Jesus left just before dark. I thought he was going to Joseph's, but he turned down a side street and a man came up to him. So I moved in real close to hear what was going on."

Toby said, "Weren't you scared?"

"Of course I was," said John Mark, "but my curiosity got the best of me, so I moved in anyway." Toby just shook his head.

John Mark went on. "Well, the man was Nicodemus, a friend of Joseph's! Also a Pharisee! And also a member of the Sanhedrin, the ruling council!" he said. "He came up to Jesus on a dark street and asked him a lot of questions. Jesus answered them, but Nicodemus didn't seem to understand the things that Jesus said."

"What happened then?" asked Toby.

"Well," began John Mark. "Jesus couldn't believe that such a scholar, a Pharisee and leader of the Jewish people, didn't understand the things he was saying. A couple of times he referred to himself as 'the Son of Man.' And then he said something I really didn't get."

"What was it?" asked Toby.

John Mark said, "He said 'the Son of Man' must be lifted up, that everyone who believes may have eternal life through him."

Toby just stared ahead and said, "Eternal life?"

"That's what he said," replied John Mark.

"Wow!" exclaimed Toby.

"But wait, that's not the best part," John Mark said. "Then Jesus said something that I'll never forget. I didn't trust myself to write it down correctly, so I memorized it, every word of it."

Toby was excited, too, and said, "Well, get to it. What was it?"

John Mark calmed himself and searched back through his memory banks, then slowly and deliberately said, "He said 'For God so loved the world that he gave his one and only son, that whoever believes in him shall have eternal life.' And he meant himself, I think! Then he just sent Nicodemus away, and I scampered back here as quick as I could." He stood up to leave. "Anyway," he said, "that's how I know certain things. And there's lots more, but I don't have time to tell you all of them right now, because I have to get over to the Temple and learn. If you come back when there's more time, I'll share them with you. Or maybe you'll just have to wait and read my stories someday," he said smiling.

"I hope I will," said Toby . . . "By the way, just out of curiosity, I know they call your mom the Widow Mary, and, well, I was just kind of wondering about your dad." John Mark stopped and looked down and sort of shook his head a little.

Toby thought he had hurt John Mark's feelings and started to apologize for being so forward, but John Mark waved him off. "When I was younger my father was killed in an accident. Pontius Pilate forced him and other men to work on construction of the aqueduct that brings water to Jerusalem. There was a terrible accident while they were digging a tunnel. Many, many men were killed in the tunnel, and my father was one of them."

John Mark seemed so sad that Toby was sorry he had asked. He placed a hand on John Mark's shoulder and said, "I'm really sorry John Mark. I know how you must feel. My dad was killed in an accident, too." John Mark said, "I guess we have a lot in common. Jesus really knew what he was doing when he brought you over to us. He must have known what good friends we'd become." Toby nodded and managed a little smile.

"In fact," said John Mark, brightening, "do you see this thing around my neck?" Toby looked at the braided necklace that held a little wooden cylinder with carvings all around it. "Yes," said Toby, "I've been admiring it. And I saw something just like it, only bigger, on the doorway into your house."

"Well this one belonged to my father," said John Mark. "It's called a mezuzah. Actually, the thing inside is really the mezuzah, but we just call the whole thing a mezuzah." John Mark lifted the necklace over his head and showed the mezuzah to Toby. It was a hollow cylinder about three inches long with decorative carving on it.

"It's beautiful," said Toby.

"Yeah, it's carved out of olive wood. Open it up! Open it up!" Toby noticed a little clasp in the middle of the mezuzah and pulled the cylinder open. Inside was a little piece of parchment with writing on it. "That's the Shema," said John Mark. "It's part of a prayer we say every day."

"What's the prayer?" asked Toby.

"It's from the Torah, our Holy Scriptures," said John Mark. "It's from the book of Deuteronomy, and it says, *Hear, O Israel: the Lord our God, the Lord is One.* The writing on the parchment is from a real Temple scribe, too. When I wear this, I not only think about God, but it also keeps my dad in my thoughts and prayers."

Toby nodded, solemnly. "That's a great way to keep your dad's memory alive," he said.

Suddenly John Mark burst into a big smile. "Hold on!" he said. "I know just what you need, Toby." He went over to his cot, reached under it, and pulled out a wooden box. "This is where I keep all my treasures," he said. He reached in and pulled out a mezuzah, just like the one around his neck, only not as fancy and on a single strand of leather, not braided like John Mark's. It was made of a dark wood and polished real smooth with some markings carved lightly along its length. "It's made of ebony wood," said John Mark. "It's not very fancy, but it has the same Shema inside."

"This is my old one," he said, "the one I wore before my mom let me have my dad's. I want you to have it."

Toby was astonished. He didn't quite know what to say. But before he could say anything John Mark held up the mezuzah and placed it around Toby's neck. John Mark then stood back with his hands on his hips and a look of immense pride on his face. "Perfect!" he exclaimed. "Now you can not only keep God's word near you, but you will also keep alive the memory of your father . . . and me, too!"

Toby was touched beyond belief. He couldn't remember anyone ever doing something so nice for him. And for no reason! Just out of friendship! He was afraid he was going to cry. He held tightly to the mezuzah, clutching it to his chest, and all he could manage to muster up was a weak "thank you" before John Mark was on the move again. "Enough of this," he cried, "I've got to get up to the Temple or I'll never write down those stories." As they went down the stairs Toby had recovered a bit, and as he followed John Mark down the stairs he said, "Gosh, if it were me I believe I'd be sleeping out there on the terrace all of the time." He smiled. "I think that I'd enjoy spying on people, too!"

John Mark pretended to be offended. "Spying?" he cried. "Spying? This is not spying, it's research!" Both boys broke out into laughter, and John Mark said, "Well, you never know, maybe you'll get your chance to sleep out there sooner rather than later." When they got downstairs John Mark left, and Toby saw Jesus in the kitchen talking to the Widow Mary. It was time to go.

As Jesus and Toby left Mary's house they crossed the road and Jesus took a steep path up the hill. Toby was confused. He said, "Hey, wait a minute, I thought we were going to Gethsemane. This isn't the way."

Jesus smiled. "You are a very alert and observant young man," he said, "but this is actually a short-cut to Gethsemane. This path winds up the back side of the Mount of Olives and along the ridge, and it will lead us directly to the Garden, only we'll be approaching it on the opposite side from what you're accustomed to."

Toby said, "Not to worry. I am the master of short-cuts!"

But then Jesus' tone turned a little more serious, and he said, "Pay very close attention to this particular short-cut, Toby, it may come in handy someday." Toby had no idea what Jesus meant, but he paid very close attention anyway.

It wouldn't be long before he'd realize just how handy this short-cut would be, for down below in the city, Jesus' enemies were already plotting to do away with him.

SECTION II

God's Kingdom Revealed

CHAPTER 6

Let the Little Children Come to Me

"Let the little children come to me, and
do not hinder them, for the Kingdom
of Heaven belongs to such as these."
Matthew 19:14

TOBY HAD A LOT TO learn about being a kid in Jesus' time. There were a lot of rules that applied to children that Toby just wasn't used to. First and foremost, children were expected to be obedient. They were expected to do what they were told to do when they were told to do it, with no questions. This was a way of showing respect, and it was very important to show adults respect.

And, boy, were children expected to work! Toby thought back to all the times his mother would ask him to do something, like clean up his room or help clear the dinner table, and he'd reply, "Hey! What am I around here, a servant or something?" Well, in Jesus' time children actually were treated a lot like servants.

When he stayed with John Mark, they would be up at the crack of dawn, before anyone else. First, they would rush into the city carrying water buckets and draw water from the community well. Then they'd haul the water back to the house for the men to use to wash up and for the women to use in their cooking and cleaning. As soon as they emptied their buckets into the household cistern, they would hike up to the wooded area outside of the city to gather kindling and firewood for the cooking fires.

While the women were baking bread, Toby and John Mark would go upstairs and help the men get dressed, lacing up their sandals or bringing them a clean tunic, and then they'd go back downstairs to fetch the men's breakfast and take it back upstairs to them. It was only after the men left that the two boys were allowed to eat their own breakfasts.

And children really were to be seen and not heard! Toby had often heard others complain that he always wanted to be the center of attention, and if he were to be totally honest, he would probably agree—a little. But in Jesus' time children got no attention. They were pretty much ignored until a grown-up wanted something. When Toby and John Mark served the men their evening meal, the two boys would sit quietly behind the men on opposite ends of the little table until someone wanted more bread, or fruit, or wine. And they had to be on their toes, too, because often the men wouldn't actually say anything. For example, a man might simply hold up his wine chalice or point to the empty space in front of him, a signal that he wanted more food. Whenever a man came to the house after traveling from another town, the two boys had to wash the man's feet, dust off his sandals, and anoint his head with a little oil. Toby began to appreciate how much better it was being a kid where he came from.

Children had to grow up quickly, too. When a boy turned thirteen he was considered an adult. Up to that point he had no rights at all; but after his Bar Mitzvah he had all the rights that any other Jewish man had. He could participate in services at the synagogue, he was counted in the census, and he could sign contracts and testify before a judge. Also included was the "right" to work in the fields or tend the sheep from dawn until dusk, just like the other adult men.

One of the main rules in Jesus' time was that children were not to talk, except when spoken to. It was considered disrespectful to simply try to start a conversation with an adult. This was the hardest rule of all for Toby. He just wasn't used to this. Apparently, he talked a lot. He didn't really think so, but it seemed like other people had commented on that pretty frequently. He also had a habit of saying whatever came into his mind at any given time. His father always called this "shooting from the lip." This particular tendency had caused him lots of problems, and because of this, other people often thought that he was rude or tactless. But he wasn't, really . . . at least he didn't think so.

And finally, people always complained that he interrupted too much, especially when he was excited. What they didn't know, though, was that he had to interrupt—if he had to wait before speaking his thought, by the time it was his turn to talk that thought would be gone. Of all the rules that children had to observe, Toby had to work the hardest on this one, especially when the men would gather in the upper room or when he was around the Disciples.

The one good thing about being ignored, though, was that the men often forgot that Toby was there altogether, and he got to listen to their conversations and stories. He started to become a pretty good source for John Mark. When John Mark had to be away from the house studying at the Temple, Toby would make it a point to remember exactly what was said and who said it so that he could relay their stories to John Mark for inclusion in the book he was going to write someday.

But when it came to children, Jesus was different from the other men. Jesus loved children. He loved their innocence, their curiosity, and the purity of their hearts. He used children as examples in his teaching, often saying that people should approach the Father as little children. He would often use the example of a father's love for his child when describing the Kingdom of Heaven and the relationship that we ought to seek with the Father.

And Jesus was always very kind to Toby, too. He didn't seem to mind if Toby asked him questions, or if he just wanted to talk a while. There were times when it seemed like Jesus actually enjoyed talking to Toby, which, for Toby, was a completely new experience. This was nice, because other grown-ups had often found Toby's questions bothersome or called him a pest for asking so many questions. But Jesus didn't seem to mind at all.

But there were other times when Toby sensed something in Jesus and just knew to be quiet. He didn't know what it was, but he knew that he needed to fight the urge to talk. There were still other times when Jesus would become very quiet and seem to be lost in his own thoughts. He would often get this faraway look in his eyes and it seemed like he was somewhere else altogether.

And then there were the times when it was clear that Jesus just needed to be by himself and have his own quiet time. Toby quickly learned when it was okay to talk and when it was best for him to keep quiet.

When Toby and Jesus were traveling together, just the two of them, Jesus always let Toby walk alongside him. But when Jesus and the Disciples traveled as a group, Toby would be off walking by himself a short ways behind the group. And when Jesus went to preach or teach or do other important things, he always had Toby sit somewhere away from what was going on. At these times Toby would usually sit in the shade of an olive tree or fig tree some distance away and just watch and listen. He didn't mind, because it was cool in the shade of the trees and he could rest his feet for a while. And besides, he really liked listening to Jesus preach.

As time went on, the crowds that followed Jesus grew larger and larger. Word spread not only about his teaching, but also of his limitless compassion, pity, and love for others. People followed him not only to hear the Word of God, but also to seek his healing touch. And because of his boundless compassion he spent a great deal of time and energy healing others. While it was certainly good that Jesus was drawing increasingly larger crowds, it also placed a greater burden and strain on him, because he would never turn anyone away who needed help or decide not to preach just because he was tired.

The Disciples were very protective of Jesus and often encouraged him to rest or to take some time off. They were tired and worn, too, and needed some time off themselves. There were times when Jesus heeded their advice, usually when he felt the need for solitude and communing with the Father. But these were few and far between. When they were in Jerusalem, though, Jesus would always retreat to the Garden of Gethsemane for prayer and contemplation.

This particular day was beautiful. There was a nice, gentle breeze coming off the water and not a cloud in the sky. But as the day wore on the breeze died down and eventually stopped altogether.

Whenever that happened the sun would just bear down and it would become terribly hot.

Jesus pointed out a place for Toby not too far away from where he was preaching. It was a nice cluster of fig trees that not only provided Toby with some much appreciated shade from the sun, but it also smelled good and provided him with a little snack of fresh ripe figs.

By the time Jesus began to preach, a huge crowd had gathered around him. As Toby looked out on the crowd he noticed that a lot of people had brought their children with them to hear Jesus, not only children around his age, but also infants and toddlers. After Jesus finished preaching, many of the parents worked their way through the crowd, begging Jesus to lay hands on their children, to bless them, and to pray for them.

But the heat had worn him down, and the Disciples knew he was tired and that he needed food and water, and most of all, to rest. So they abruptly turned the children away. They felt that Jesus simply didn't have the time or the energy to be bothered with a bunch of kids right now.

Jesus was indeed tired, very tired. And he, too, knew he needed to rest. But unlike most people in his time, he loved the little children and he wanted them to know it. He refused to let them be turned away, and was determined not to make them feel rejected or unworthy of his attentions. He immediately stopped what he was doing and sternly, in a very loud, no-nonsense voice, told the Disciples to stop turning the children away and to let them through.

Toby had been quietly sitting under the fig trees just a little distance away while Jesus was teaching. He had listened for a while, but soon he just drifted off, daydreaming. He was startled out of his reverie when he heard Jesus raise his voice and get very stern with his men. That didn't happen very often, and it captured Toby's attention. He looked up and heard Jesus instructing the men to stand back and let the children come unto him. As the children began moving toward him, Jesus turned his head ever so slightly and gave a little nod in Toby's direction.

Well, Toby didn't have to be told twice! He jumped up and ran as fast as he could and joined the crowd of children gathered at Jesus' feet. Jesus smiled at the children and then looked at the men who had tried to keep them away. He said, "Suffer the little children to come unto me, and do not hinder them, for the Kingdom of God belongs to such as these."

The Kingdom of God, thought Toby, *it belongs to such as me—such as me! Awesome!*

When Jesus finished talking he took the children one by one in his arms and hugged and blessed each one of them. Toby was the last one in line. But even though he was last, he was certain that Jesus hugged him just a little tighter and just a little bit longer than all the others. He usually wasn't too crazy about being hugged, but he found himself wishing that this one would never end. He had never felt so safe, so warm, or so loved, not in his entire life.

He held on tight to his mezuzah and made sure to remember this event in every single detail so that John Mark could write it down someday. Especially that part about *such as me!*

The Kingdom of Heaven

"Repent for the Kingdom of Heaven is at hand."
Matthew 3:2

J UST THE OTHER DAY JESUS was teaching the Disciples and a huge crowd gathered around them. The crowd was so large that Jesus walked halfway up the mount and began to preach to them. Now, Toby loved Jesus, of that there was no doubt. But it seemed like everything that Jesus said was just about the opposite of the way Toby felt.

As Jesus began to preach he looked out at the crowd and said, "Blessed be the poor, for theirs is the Kingdom of Heaven."

Well, ever since Toby's dad died his mom had to work hard, sometimes at two jobs. There were often things they couldn't do because they didn't have the money. They lost their house and had to move to a rougher part of the neighborhood. Toby had to go home to an empty apartment every day because his mom was working and couldn't afford for him to be in the after-school program with his friends. No, Toby didn't see anything at all "blessed" about that. In fact, he thought that being poor kind of stunk.

Then he heard Jesus say, "Blessed are those who mourn, for they will be comforted."

Wrong again, thought Toby. *I've been mourning ever since my dad died. Every day. And so has my mom. Sometimes it seems like we haven't done anything but mourn. And I haven't been comforted one little bit!* He thought that mourning kind of stunk, too.

But then Toby was jolted out of this thought when he heard Jesus say, "Blessed are the meek, for they will inherit the earth."

Not in my neighborhood, Toby thought. *In my neighborhood you'd see pretty quick what being "meek" would get you. All you'd inherit by being meek is a fat lip or a black eye.*

Jesus went on to say, "Blessed are those who thirst for righteousness, for they will be filled," and then, "Blessed are the merciful, for they will be shown mercy." But Toby was still stuck back on the "virtues" of being meek. Besides, he wasn't even sure he knew what "righteousness" was. And that "merciful" thing took him right back to being meek. He hadn't seen a lot of people showing others mercy, and he wasn't sure he wanted to find out what would happen to him if he did.

Then Jesus said, "Blessed are the pure of heart, for they will see God." Toby paid little attention to this one, because he didn't think that he could ever be "pure of heart," and he chuckled to himself thinking that he wasn't really sure he'd want to see God. He'd read about people that God had talked to, and they seemed to have nothing but trouble. He could only imagine what might happen to you if you were to actually see God.

Then he heard: "Blessed are the peacemakers for they will be called the children of God."

Toby couldn't help but think that Jesus must have grown up in a nice neighborhood, because he didn't think there were any peacemakers in his. Not that he'd seen, anyway.

Then came the icing on the cake. Jesus said, "Blessed are you when people insult you, persecute you and falsely say all kinds of evil against you because of me. Rejoice and be glad, because great is your reward in heaven, for in the same way they persecuted the prophets who were before you."

Well, by now Toby was just shaking his head. He had felt certainly persecuted at times, and he felt like people were all the time "falsely saying all kinds of evil" against him. *And I'll tell you one thing, too,* thought Toby, *it never made me feel like rejoicing and being glad. No sir, not once.* In fact, it had made him bitter and angry and left him wanting to do nothing other than to find ways of getting back at them.

After that Jesus sat down, as was a rabbi's custom when teaching, and he spoke to the crowd for a long, long time. Toby didn't understand all of what Jesus said, but there were a number of things he did understand, and he found himself getting more and more uncomfortable.

Jesus had said, "You have heard that it was said 'an eye for an eye and a tooth for a tooth.'" Now, Toby knew from Sunday School what this meant. It meant if someone did something to you, you turn around and do the same thing to them. He got that.

But then Jesus said, "But I say to you do not resist an evil person. If anyone strikes you on the right cheek, turn to them the other cheek also. And if anyone wants to take your shirt, hand over your coat as well. If someone makes you go one mile, go with him two miles. Give to the one who asks you, and do not turn away from the one who wants to borrow from you."

This still wasn't making much sense to Toby. *How can you expect someone not to fight back*, he thought. *Word gets out that you don't fight back and the next thing you know, you're a target for every bully on the block.* No sir, Toby had always given it right back to them. As he reflected on this, he was kind of embarrassed to realize that there were also times when he had actually been the one doing the bullying. But he told himself that he had to do this every now and then or everyone would think he was a sissy. Best defense is a good offense, after all, right?

Jesus continued: "You have heard that it was said, 'Love your neighbor and hate your enemy.' But I tell you, love your enemies and pray for those who persecute you, that you may be children of your Father in heaven."

Well, this was just getting to be too much. Toby was amazed at how Jesus could have gotten it so wrong. But there was this nagging little thought in the back of his mind. He tried to push it away but the more he tried, the more it grew and grew until it reached full bloom, right there in front of him. He thought he might have felt his heart stop as he fully understood what had been nagging at him:

What if it wasn't Jesus who got it so wrong? After all, if it came between him and Jesus as to who got things right and who got things wrong, well . . .

Toby began to sense that he might be in a bit of trouble here. This thought stayed with him all through the afternoon and into the evening.

The group was staying in a familiar place near Capernaum. Toby had been here many times before. Atop the hill was a large clearing, and on the hillside near the cave where everyone slept was a sharp outcropping of large rocks that overlooked a lush, green valley below. One of Toby's favorite things was to crawl up to the top of the largest one and sit so he could see the entire valley below him. He called it his "thinking rock" because it was a peaceful place where he could get away from everything and be by himself. He often used this time to think about the events of the day and to organize the things he would relate to John Mark the next time he saw him. When the group traveled through Capernaum they went from place to place during the day, but most nights they would make their way back to this spot, and Toby would almost always spend time on his thinking rock.

This particular evening Toby felt at peace sitting atop his rock, although he still had that nagging thought in his head. It was getting dark, and while he couldn't see the valley anymore, he could lie back on the rock and look at the stars in the heavens. He knew that Jesus liked this spot, too, and there were times that Jesus would come here at the end of the day and talk a little. Toby hoped that this would be one of those evenings.

And he wasn't disappointed, for very soon Jesus appeared in the moonlight. He stood very still, his face turned to the stars, and he seemed to be saying something. Toby had come to understand that this usually meant that Jesus was praying or communing in some way with the Father. After a few moments Jesus made his way over to the rock and quietly sat beside Toby. For the longest time neither one said anything. Toby got the sense that Jesus was waiting for him to say something, but he didn't know what to say.

He didn't have to say anything, though. Jesus obviously already knew. Finally, Jesus said, "Toby, I can tell there's something on your mind. What is it?"

Toby tried to brush off Jesus' question, saying "Oh, you know, nothing really, just the regular stuff, nothing in particular."

Jesus smiled. "Toby, by now I would have thought you would have realized that I know you better than that. Come on, now, let's hear it."

Toby thought for a moment, then said, "I don't know, it just seemed like a lot of the things . . . Well, I listened to you talking today, and a lot of the things you said were 'blessed.' Well . . . don't take this the wrong way or anything, but I guess I'm not so sure that they really are. 'Blessed,' that is. In fact, some of them just kind of stink . . . no offense."

"None taken," smiled Jesus. The two sat in silence for what seemed to Toby to be a long time. Long enough to make him uncomfortable, anyway. Then Jesus turned and looked at Toby with great sympathy. "I can see why you might feel that way," he said. "Toby, make no mistake—there's nothing 'blessed' about being poor, or being persecuted, not at all. Those are painful conditions, and you wouldn't wish them on anyone." He looked up at the stars and said, "The real point is that the cares of this world pale in comparison to the riches in the world to come. Poverty is no blessing, to be sure. But those who endure their poverty with humility and dignity and who maintain their faith in my Father despite their poverty are surely blessed, for they will find riches beyond their wildest dreams in the world to come."

"And the Father's heart breaks for those who mourn, for those who experience great loss. And it breaks for you in your loss and mourning. Even though people who mourn may not find comfort in this realm, if they maintain their faith despite their considerable sadness, great peace and comfort will be theirs in the world to come. They will rest in the arms of the Father."

"Well, how about the meek?" asked Toby. "There's not much payoff for that, is there?"

Jesus was quick to say, "Maybe not in this realm, but in the world to come there will be payoff aplenty. To be meek doesn't mean to be a sissy—it means to be humble, to trust in God's strength rather than in your own." Jesus continued: "And if you thirst and hunger for righteousness, if you strive to be like the Father the way a starving man strives for food or a thirsty man strives for water, you will never thirst or be hungry in the world to come. If you show others mercy in this realm, you will be shown unlimited mercy in the world to come. Likewise, if you strive for peace, if you try to settle conflicts with others in this realm, you will find eternal peace in the world to come. And finally, if you cleanse your heart in this realm, if you are pure of heart, you will see God."

Toby said, "What does that mean, you'll see God?"

"Well," said Jesus, "you'll see the Father in this world, because if your heart is pure you will be like God, and you will see God in your actions. And in the world to come you will be with God, in every sense of the word. He will hold you in the palm of His hand."

Toby glanced sideways at Jesus, and said, quietly, "I noticed you haven't said anything about that 'persecution' thing, what about that? How great can that be?"

Jesus sighed deeply, and a look of sadness came upon his face. He shook his head slowly and said, "Toby, there is evil in this realm. The prince of this world is afoot."

Toby was startled. "Satan, you mean?" he said.

"Satan," said Jesus, nodding. "And Satan is not just a being— Satan is the very embodiment of all the evil in the world. And there's a battle coming I'm afraid. A battle between the forces of good and the forces of evil. There are those in Jerusalem who seek to hurt me, even to kill me. This I understand, for it is all part of the Father's plan. But sadly, there will also be those who will seek to hurt the ones who believe in me, just because they believe in me. The Father wants all believers to know that if they maintain their faith, even if they are ridiculed, despised, and persecuted because of me, they will find their reward in the world to come. In the world to come, you see, they will be one with him."

There were more long moments of silence. Finally, Toby said, "So it's all about keeping your eyes on the prize, right?"

Jesus couldn't help but laugh. "You never cease to amaze me, Toby," he said. "Probably not the exact words I would have chosen, but you're right on the mark. Yes, keeping your eyes on the prize."

"Well," said Toby, "what words would you use?"

Jesus thought for a moment. "I suppose the way I would put it is to make sure to place your love of God the Father above everything else. Everything else. And especially the cares of this world. Greed, false pride, selfishness, anger, lust, striving for material wealth, all these things are very appealing in this world. So appealing that they can threaten to crowd God out of your heart. But if you truly keep your love of the Father first and foremost in your heart, the cares of this world will be bearable because you will be included in Heaven's Reign."

Toby smiled, very pleased with himself that he "got" it. But the more he thought about it, the more troubled he became. Jesus saw the worry on Toby's face. "What is it?" he asked.

After a long silence Toby said, "I don't know, it's just that . . . it's just that all the things you said we should do . . . well . . . I guess I didn't do them . . . haven't done them . . . don't do them . . . never have done them, really . . . not even sure that I can do them." Toby sighed. "I suppose it just seems that you want people to be perfect or something. I think I even heard you say that, right?"

"It's complicated, Toby," Jesus said. "The Father created you in His image, and more than anything He wants you to strive to be like Him. Now, He's perfect, and obviously man is not. But that's not what counts. What counts is that you try. What counts is that you strive to be more like Him every day. That you keep Him foremost in your heart and in your thoughts at all times. The fact that you'll come up short is just a reminder to keep you humble and to help you keep in mind how much you need to depend on Him. He wants these things for you because He loves you. And He wants you to understand that His love is more valuable than all the riches in the world. More valuable than all the worldly power you could amass. More valuable than anything you could ever achieve in this realm.

And when you show this very same love to others, you are seeing Him, because He is that love."

With that, Jesus got up and went to join the others. Toby stayed on his thinking rock, staring up at the stars. As he pondered what Jesus had said he began to look at things in a different light. He thought about how much his dad had loved him and the things they had shared together. He thought about his dad's parents and how his grandma's house always smelled so good and how his granddad would always slip him candy and tell him not to tell grandma. He thought about his mom's parents and how her father would take him fishing or to ball games and how much they would laugh when they were together. He thought about her mother and how she always cooked the best meals, and how she always seemed to give him just a little extra desert. He thought about how much fun it was when the whole family got together and he got to see all his cousins. He also thought about his friends and coaches and teachers who had meant something to him.

And mostly he thought about his mom. He thought about the sacrifices she had made for him. Even though she worked two jobs, she always seemed to be able to make some time for him. She read to him every night as she put him to bed, even though she was really tired. She would play games with him after homework time and make sure he got his bath and brushed his teeth. And she was up early every morning so she could wake him, and she always made him breakfast. All of this. Just because she loved him.

As Toby fell asleep atop his thinking rock he found himself thinking that maybe he wasn't so poor after all. In fact, in that moment he felt pretty rich . . . and very lucky. And very much loved.

CHAPTER 8

The Healings

"Jesus went through all the towns and villages, teaching in their synagogues, proclaiming the good news of the kingdom and healing every disease and sickness."

Matthew 9:35

FOR THE NEXT BIT OF time the group traveled back to the north of Palestine to Galilee. Jesus' home town, Nazareth, was also in Galilee. Jesus spent a great deal of time teaching, preaching, and healing all manner of sick people in and around Galilee. Toby was amazed at the things his friend could do.

There was this horrible disease called leprosy, and people that had it were treated very badly. They weren't allowed to touch anyone, and often they weren't even allowed to be near other people. Now, to be honest, Toby didn't think this was such a bad idea. These people had ugly sores and boils all over their skin, and they smelled really bad. So he could sort of understand why people shunned them and made them stay away.

But the Jews shunned them for other reasons. They believed that if you were righteous, God would reward you, and if you were wicked and sinful he would punish you. So, they viewed sickness and infirmity as something you brought on yourself by not behaving the way you're supposed to. They shunned these people not only because they looked horrible and smelled bad, but also because they believed them to be wicked and sinful.

But apparently Jesus felt differently. One day a man with leprosy came running up to Jesus. The man fell down on his knees at
Jesus' feet and said, "Lord, I know that you can cure me, if you are
willing." Everyone else, including Toby, was moving far away from
this man, afraid he might make them sick. But Jesus didn't flinch. He
stood right there and looked at the man, and you could tell that it
was with love in his heart. He could see into the man's heart and he
knew that the man had great faith.

Jesus closed his eyes and said, "I am willing; be cured."

And he was! Just like that!

Soon afterward they were walking down the road and Toby
spied a Roman soldier coming toward them. This usually wasn't
good, because the Romans ruled over Jesus' people, and they could
be pretty mean sometimes. But this soldier was different. His servant,
whom he loved, was ill, and he believed that Jesus could heal the
man. Toby thought this could be a trick. He had never heard of a
Roman who cared at all about his servants. Servants were essentially
slaves—if one got sick and died, you simply got yourself another one
to replace him. Yep, Toby was pretty sure this was trickery.

But apparently Jesus didn't. Toby didn't know it, but Jesus had
looked into the soldier's heart and had seen that he, too, had great
faith. He asked the soldier where his house was. Toby was afraid that
going to the Roman's house would be walking right into a trap! He
was just about to say something when the soldier said, "Lord, you
don't need to come to my house. I have faith that if you say he is
healed, he will be healed." Well, now Toby was confused. But he was
still pretty sure this was a trick of some sort. Then when he saw Jesus
smile, he figured the jig was up and they were all about to share a
good laugh.

But Jesus' smile meant something else. Jesus was smiling because
he was so pleased and amazed at the depth of this man's faith. He was
surprised that the faith of a Roman soldier would be greater than that
of even many of his Disciples. The desert wind blew gently as Jesus
bowed his head and said a silent prayer. He opened his eyes, quietly
blessed the soldier, and told him to return home where he would find
his servant alive and well. The centurion left and the group contin-

ued on their journey. Shortly thereafter a messenger came running up to them breathlessly praising Jesus and telling them that indeed the servant had been healed.

Then there was a woman who had been bleeding for over ten years. No doctor had ever been able to help her, and she had just about given up all hope. But she still had great faith in God, and when she heard about Jesus she had great faith in him as well. She came to believe that if she could just touch the hem of Jesus' robe she would be healed.

When she heard that Jesus and his Disciples were coming to her village she was determined to see him. But by the time she got to the outskirts of the village a huge crowd had already gathered around the men, and she could barely see Jesus. She didn't see how she could possibly reach Jesus through this throng of people, but pushed onward by her faith, she weaved her way through the crowd. The closer she got, the thicker the crowd was. She kept on pushing through, but just when she got barely close enough to reach him, she was jostled and knocked to the ground. She was determined, though, and through the legs of those near Jesus she could see his feet and the bottom of his tunic. She steeled herself, and with all her might she stretched her arm out as far as it would go, reaching toward the hem of Jesus' garment.

She touched it! And at that very instant she knew it! She could feel it! She was completely cured!

Jesus stopped abruptly. He looked around at the crowd. Then he said that he felt some power leave from him and asked who had touched him. The woman was terrified and said nothing. He continued to survey the crowd and again asked who had touched him. The woman's faith overcame her fear, and she meekly approached him, saying that she was the one.

Everyone, including Toby, was certain that Jesus was really going to let her have it. Not only was she a woman, and in Jesus' time women had to "know their place," but she was also unclean because of the bleeding. They were certain that Jesus would be angry with her for daring to touch him.

She bowed her head and told Jesus why she had touched his robe. She, too, was afraid he would be angry with her, and she bowed her head and knelt before him. But instead of being angry, he was very kind to her. Jesus looked at her, and Toby saw that same smile again. Jesus quietly said something to her, blessed her, and sent her along her way.

As Toby watched all these things he was amazed at Jesus' powers. He began to feel kind of envious. He couldn't help but wonder how great it would be if he had that kind of power. This thought excited him. Why, if he had this kind of power he could get back at all the people that had made him mad. He could have just about anything he wanted. He began to daydream about how all the other kids would think he was so awesome if he had such powers. Why, he would be just like a celebrity!

So you can imagine his surprise and shock when it dawned on him that Jesus never took credit for these things. When Jesus healed the man with leprosy, he told him not to tell anyone. Instead, he told him to go to the synagogue and pray. When he healed the centurion's servant he told the soldier that it was the strength of his faith that had healed his servant. And he didn't even take credit for healing the woman with perpetual bleeding. When he spoke to her he said, "Daughter, your faith has healed you. Go in peace and suffer no more."

Faith. This whole notion of faith had kind of stumped Toby. One evening when Jesus came back from praying, he found Toby sitting atop his thinking rock in the dark. It was a clear, crisp desert night, and a gentle wind was rustling through the leaves of the olive trees. Toby was looking up at the stars. Jesus climbed up the rock and quietly sat down next to Toby.

After a very long silence Toby said, "There must be a billion of them up there!" Jesus looked up at the heavens and just quietly smiled. "I've been thinking about what you said to those people that you made better," Toby said.

"Refresh my memory," said Jesus. "I said a lot of things."

"The thing about faith, and how it was really their faith that made them whole and that cured the soldier's servant," Toby said.

"It's a word I've heard a lot in church, and I've even used it before. But I have to tell you, I'm not sure what it really means." After a pause he added, "And I really don't get how faith healed those people."

"Ah, faith," Jesus said. "Let me think about this for a minute." He looked up in the sky and said, "When you wake up tomorrow, will you be able to see these stars, Toby?"

Toby said, "Of course not, you can't see them when it's light outside. Anybody knows that."

Jesus smiled. "And so tomorrow if I ask you if the stars are still up in the sky, what will you tell me?"

Toby looked confused, but after a few moments he slowly grinned. "Okay, okay, I see where you're going with this," he said. "Of course I'll believe that they're still there."

"Well," Jesus said, "faith is a lot like that. Faith is being convinced that something is true, even though you can't prove that it's true. Faith is having complete trust that something is real, even though you can't touch it or see it." He paused a little bit, and then said, "Faith means believing in God . . . and it means believing that the things I say and do are a reflection of His will, that God really does these things through me."

"Then why don't you tell everybody that!" exclaimed Toby. "Gosh, if it were me, I'd be shouting it from the rooftops! I'd say, 'Hey, people, God's working through me—through me! Better listen up!' You know? But you keep it secret. You don't tell anyone. Even when Peter said that you were the true Messiah, the Son of God, you told him not to tell anybody, even though you really are. When you were on the mountaintop and you stood there actually speaking with Moses and Elijah, even then, you told Peter and James and John not to tell anyone. I don't get it."

Jesus' mood became serious. "You don't miss a thing, do you, Toby?" he asked. He stood, moved around the rock as if deep in thought, and then stopped and said, "Do you remember over in Cana, at the wedding, when I was asked to help when the wine ran out?"

"Yes," said Toby. "At first you said you wouldn't do it, and then you did."

"Do you remember what I said?" asked Jesus.

'Toby thought for a moment, then said, "Yes, yes I do. You said something about it wasn't 'your hour' yet or something like that."

"That is correct," said Jesus.

But before he could go on Toby interrupted him. "And I remember you telling us about when your brothers were taunting you, they were teasing you and telling you to go to Jerusalem for the feast and show your mighty works in public. Again, at first you said no but then you went anyway. You said something like that then, too."

Jesus' eyebrows raised in surprise. "My goodness, Toby, when I picked you to be my helper I had no idea what a sharp mind you have. Sometimes you truly amaze me." Toby beamed. "And you're right, Jude and James were chiding me, pushing me to go to Jerusalem and perform miracles for all the public to see. I told them that it was not yet my time; and they left me alone."

"So, what does all of that mean?" asked Toby.

"Well Toby," said Jesus, "the Jews have been waiting for the Messiah for over a thousand years. But they're just not ready to accept him yet. They expect the Messiah to be someone like their King David, the greatest warrior king Israel has ever known. They expect the Messiah to come like a great commanding general and lead an army to overthrow the Romans and restore Israel to her favored status among nations. I'm afraid the last thing they expect is someone like me. Someone who tells them to turn the other cheek, to love their enemies, to pray for those who hate them, and to pay their taxes to their Roman oppressors." Toby was slowly nodding his head.

Jesus continued: "So, timing is important. I need to move these people to a position of letting go of their notions of the Messiah so that they can then accept the true Messiah. The miracles I perform aren't for show. They're not like some kind of magic trick. They are divine revelations—demonstrations of the nature of God's love, and His mercy. These revelations need time to sink in so that people can really see them for what they are, and then they will be better able to see me for who I am. Rest assured, though, when the time is right, I'll let them know exactly who I am and whose power is responsible for these miracles. And you'll be right there with me. You won't miss a thing. You just have to have faith."

"Faith," muttered Toby. Jesus looked over at him and saw *that look*. That bewildered, perplexed look that Toby always gets when he's trying really hard to understand something difficult, but just not getting very far with it. After a moment Toby simply shrugged and asked, "Okay, so, faith. I want to have it. How do I go about getting some? And how will I know if I've got it or not?"

Jesus laughed and laughed, and then he looked at Toby with his own *that look*—that look in his eyes that shows his boundless love and kindness. That look. That look that shows bottomless sympathy and compassion. That look that makes you feel like he can see right inside of you, right into your heart.

Jesus' eyes twinkled a bit, and he gently said, "Oh, you'll know, my friend. Trust me, you'll know. Perhaps sooner than you may think." Then he stood and said, "To bed with you now, we have a big, big day tomorrow." Toby took one last look at the stars, then climbed down off the rock and went right to sleep.

CHAPTER 9

Serving Others

"Here is a boy with five small barley loaves and two small fish, but how
far will they go among so many?"

John 6:9

ESUS AND HIS DISCIPLES WERE all very tired and needed a rest. They all needed to get away for a while, for a little peace and quiet, some prayer and reflection. The crowds following Jesus had been growing larger and larger, and it was hard to go anywhere without drawing a crowd. These people were very needy, and Jesus couldn't help but feel compassion for them. So he never turned anyone away. But he's just a man, after all, and he felt a need to get away from them for a little while. So in the morning they all boarded Peter's fishing boat and sailed to the far shore of the Sea of Galilee.

But it didn't work. Word of Jesus' teachings and his healing had reached far and wide. When people saw him leaving, many ran around the end of the Sea of Galilee and got there before he did. And when the people on the far shore heard that he was coming, the word spread like wildfire. People gathered around from all of the many towns in that region and rushed to the shore. They wanted to see Jesus when he landed. By the time Jesus and the Disciples arrived, the crowd was huge, about five thousand by some estimates, far more than that by others.

When the Disciples saw the size of the crowd that had gathered they were dismayed. They were tired and hungry, and were looking forward to some "down time." They also knew that Jesus wouldn't turn his back on the crowd. When they voiced their concerns, Jesus looked upon the crowd with compassion in his eyes. He said they were like sheep without a shepherd, lost and in need of spiritual nourishment. So as he always did, he left the boat and walked over to a hillside. He spent a good deal of time healing the various sick and afflicted members of the crowd, and then went higher up on the hillside and spoke to them for quite a while.

When they were boarding the boat earlier that day, Jesus had called Toby over to him. He said that he had an important task for him. Toby was thrilled. He was eager to help in any way he could. Jesus walked him over to the other side of the road where he saw a small blanket draped over something. Jesus lifted the blanket and Toby saw a woven basket, and in it were five loaves of bread and two fish, salted and dried.

Toby looked disappointed. Jesus looked at him and said, "What is it, Toby?" Toby shook off his disappointment and said, "Nothing . . . nothing at all." But Jesus would not be put off so easily. He asked again, "Toby, I can tell by the look on your face that something is wrong. What is it?"

Toby looked down at the basket, a little embarrassed. "When you said you had something important for me to do, I just thought maybe it was something really important. Something more important than . . . well, something a little more important than just carrying a basket with my lunch in it."

Jesus looked directly at him and said, "Trust me, Toby. This task is a little more important than simply carrying your lunch." Then he leaned down and whispered, "Now you take this basket and don't let it out of your sight. And don't lift the blanket or uncover it for any reason, not until I tell you to."

Toby was still a little disappointed, but he shrugged and sort of dejectedly said, "Okay, whatever you say."

Jesus stopped him and said, "I want you to listen carefully. This is important. Now, when we get to the other shore I want you to take the basket and go find a quiet, shady place to rest until I need you. You just keep an eye on me, and I'll let you know when I need you."

Toby nodded. He thought to himself that he was getting really good at finding shady places to rest while Jesus and the others did "important" things, so he slowly started walking away.

Jesus sensed Toby's disappointment and maybe a little resentment as well. He called him back and together they sat on a rock wall. Jesus was silent for a few moments, but then he turned and looked Toby right in the eye and said, almost sternly, "Listen to me, young man. No job is too small in the eyes of the Father. Your job is just as important as anything the others will do, and don't you forget it. Any task done out of love for the Father, no matter how small or unimportant you may think it is, is a great, great accomplishment, and is valued by the Father. Remember this and be proud of whatever you do in His name."

Toby got the message. He sheepishly looked up at Jesus and said, "I'm sorry . . . I guess I was just thinking about myself and how much I'd like to feel important, too."

Jesus said, "Toby, in God's eyes you are more important than you could ever know. He knows everything about you. He knows your comings and your goings, your restings and your risings, right down to how many hairs are on your head." Toby got *that look* again, but he smiled nonetheless. Even if he didn't understand everything that Jesus said, he got the point.

Jesus smiled and said, "Now go do your job. And do it well." Toby turned and as he walked over to the tree he began to stand a little straighter and walk with a little more purpose. He smiled. It felt good to know he was important to God.

By the time Jesus finished preaching it was getting late. The Disciples hadn't eaten in a long time, and they were getting a bit cranky. They said to Jesus, "This is a remote place, and it is getting late. Send the people away so they can go to the villages and buy themselves something to eat."

But Jesus had compassion for the crowd. He said, "They do not need to go away. I want you to give them something to eat." The one called Phillip stood up and shouted, "That would take over half a year's wages for each one to have just a bite. Are we to go and spend that much on bread and give it to them to eat?"

Jesus calmly, but firmly said, "We shall feed them."

Just as Jesus said this, the one called Andrew spotted Toby sitting under a tree with his basket. He walked over, lifted the blanket and saw the loaves and fishes. He turned to Jesus and said, "Here is a boy with five small barley loaves and two fishes, but how far will they go among so many?" Jesus looked at Toby and nodded slightly, and Toby got the sense that something big was afoot. Something great was about to happen.

Jesus gathered his Disciples around him and calmly addressed them. He told them to go into the crowd and to assemble the people into groups of fifty to one hundred each across the hillside. Toby watched as the men obediently did as they were told. When they returned from this task he pointed out a fig tree, and under this fig tree were a number of baskets. He gathered the men around him and then called to Toby. Toby stood at attention. Jesus instructed him to bring his basket front and center. Toby beamed and ran over there as fast as he could. He handed the basket over to Jesus and sat on the ground in front of him.

Jesus took the loaves into his hands, closed his eyes, and held them up toward the heavens. He blessed the bread and said a prayer, giving thanks to the Father for the bounty He had provided them. He then took the fish and did the same thing.

After giving thanks, Jesus began breaking the loaves into pieces. He then instructed Toby to place the pieces of the bread into each Disciple's basket. Then he did the same with the fishes. Toby was excited over playing such an important role in this situation, but he couldn't get rid of this nagging feeling that this whole thing was a little crazy. This was just five loaves and two fishes, for goodness' sake. How in the world could he feed so many people with so little food? He began to feel a little embarrassed for Jesus. What would the crowd do when they realized there was no food? But he set these concerns aside and did as he was told.

The Disciples left. After a while Toby could see them on the hillside, weaving their way through the crowd and carrying their baskets, going from one group to another. Toby expected them to run out any minute now. But they never stopped! They just kept going from group to group to group until the last person had been fed! After they had fed everyone, they began making their way back to Jesus, and the crowd began to disperse. The people started on their journeys back to their towns so that they could get home before nightfall. As the Disciples gathered around Jesus, he told them that now they were free to eat as much as they needed from their baskets. After they had eaten he sent them back over to the hillside to gather in the crumbs and morsels that the crowd left behind. They returned with the twelve baskets, and everyone was filled to the brim with food! Amazing! Toby had never seen such a thing in his entire life.

Jesus began walking away from the Disciples. He spotted Toby and gave a little nod. Toby ran over to him and began to walk beside him. Together they walked over a small hill toward a large stand of olive trees. Toby was beside himself with excitement and was just dying to ask Jesus all about this wondrous miracle. But as they walked he glanced over at Jesus, and he knew that this was one of those times. This was one of those times when he could sense that Jesus needed some quiet, some alone time. So despite his excitement, he didn't say a word.

As they neared the olive grove Jesus stopped and sat on the ground, and he told Toby to do the same. Toby thought *This is it! This is when he lets me in on the secret! This is when he tells me what happened out there!* But Jesus had already put the feeding of the five thousand behind him. He was looking forward, not backward. He had other things on his mind.

He looked at Toby, and Toby could see how tired he was. He smiled gently at Toby and said, "I told you that your job was important, didn't I?"

Toby beamed, and said, "No task is too small if it honors the Father, right?"

Jesus smiled again, and said, "Right you are, my friend." Then he added, "And maybe you should keep this in mind the next time you are asked to help the older folks in your congregation on Sunday afternoons." Toby's mouth hung open as he wondered how Jesus knew about that! Who could have told him? Then Jesus smiled gently, rose, and silently walked away to speak to the Disciples.

And Toby got the message.

CHAPTER 10

Faith

"Truly I tell you, if you have faith as small as
a mustard seed, you can say to this mountain,
'Move from here to there,' and it will move.
Nothing will be impossible for you."

Matthew 17:20

AFTER THE MIRACLE OF FEEDING the five thousand, the Disciples
were amazed. They were chattering excitedly among themselves
about what they had witnessed. Despite their fatigue, they were
excited. They wanted to celebrate this event and talk all about it
with Jesus. But Jesus was tired. He wasn't interested in chatter. He
instructed the Disciples to go back to the boat and set sail for the
town they had left this morning. He told them he would meet them
tomorrow in the town on the other shore. So they boarded the fishing boat and set out back across the Sea of Galilee.

As the group set sail, Jesus went back to get Toby and together
they headed toward a very thick, dense grove of olive trees. As they
neared the olive grove Jesus nodded in that direction and said, "I
need to go in there where it's quiet. I need to feel the presence of the
Father. I may be in there quite a while, because when I pray I don't
just say a little prayer that I memorized as a child. When I pray, I pray
long and hard. I praise God, and I thank Him for His mercy and
grace. And I also spend time listening, listening quietly. And in the
still quiet I open up my heart to the Father. It is in those still, quiet

moments that His presence can be felt, and right now I need that. I need to feel His presence."

Toby was amazed that Jesus would talk to him about such personal things. He nodded solemnly and asked what Jesus would have him do in the meantime.

Jesus pointed toward a small, but dense grouping of fig trees just a little ways away and said, "In that grove you'll find a little spot that's been made ready for you. The blanket from your basket of food is in there. You need to rest. I want you to go in there and go to sleep until I come for you." Then he smiled and said, "You and I have a lot of ground to cover before morning. You'll need your rest."

Well, Toby didn't have to be told twice. He made his way over to the fig trees and worked his way into the center. There he found the bed that was waiting for him, and he was asleep before his head hit the blanket.

Several hours later Jesus gently awakened Toby. It was pitch black. Toby couldn't see a thing. He grabbed his blanket and had to feel his way out of the fig trees. He could barely see in front of his face. "Boy, is it ever dark," he said. "Clouds must have covered the moon and all the stars." After a brief pause he laughed and said, "But I still believe they're there, even though I can't see them, right? I have faith." Although Toby couldn't see Jesus' face, he knew that Jesus would be smiling.

As they began walking Jesus said, "Take my hand, Toby," and Toby did. After a few moments Jesus said, "We've got a long way to go and the weather isn't cooperating very well. You can see how dark it is. That means there's a major storm brewing, and we can't avoid it. We're going to have to put our heads down and get to where we're going despite the storm."

As they walked a little farther the wind started to pick up. Toby could feel the gusts of wind trying to push him this way and that, and he began to get a little worried. But after a few moments Jesus slowed his pace a little, and then stopped walking altogether. Toby couldn't see his face, but he knew Jesus was looking right at him.

"You need to listen closely to me, Toby, because this is very, very important," he said. "This storm is building, and it's going to be a fierce one. Now, I'm going to hold onto your hand as long as I can. But there will be times when I won't be able to. There'll be some things that I have to do, and I'll have to do them without you. So, when I tell you to let go, you let go. No questions asked. You'll just have to do as I say and trust that I'll keep you near and safe, and that I'll be there for you, no matter what."

Toby was still afraid. But this time there was something different. Unlike other times when he'd been afraid, this time there was a sense of calm deep down inside of him. In spite of his fear, somehow he just knew everything would be all right. He stiffened his resolve and silently nodded, saying nothing. Jesus sensed that Toby was ready. He gave his hand a squeeze, a signal they were ready to move, and off they went into the darkness.

Toby noticed that at times the ground seemed to shift under his feet. He could tell they were walking down the same grassy hillside where he and the Disciples had fed the five thousand. He could tell when they left the hillside and were on a rocky road or lane.

Once they came down from the hillside the wind really seemed to pick up, and Toby was thinking about what Jesus had said about the storm that was brewing. Then, all of a sudden the ground began to feel completely different. No more hillside. No more rocks. No more uneven ground. The ground beneath his feet felt smooth as silk, flat as a pancake, and not very hard at all.

But the farther they went the more the wind picked up. All of a sudden he felt great *whooshes* of wind as it gusted more and more. He felt the ground under his feet begin to feel less stable, moving up and down rapidly, like it was moving with the wind. He felt like he was being moved by forces beyond his control, and he began to feel scared. He started to ask where they were, and just what the heck they were doing, but he remembered what Jesus had said and kept his thoughts to himself. Almost as though he could sense Toby's anxiety, Jesus quietly said, "We're on our way to meet up with the others. They set sail this morning, and we're going to meet them on the other side. I know these winds are fierce, but we have to keep moving ahead. We've still got a ways to go."

Toby just kept plodding along. The wind was growing fiercer all the time and the ground under his feet continued to move erratically, but he just kept his head down and kept walking. Soon he was lost in thought, kind of in a daze, and time just slipped away.

Jesus suddenly brought him back to reality. He abruptly stopped and said, "Toby, let go of my hand, but keep walking."

Toby became very much afraid and grasped Jesus' hand tighter. "But . . . but . . . but Jesus, the wind is howling and it's so dark I can barely see. Please don't just turn me loose."

But Jesus was firm, saying, "Toby, you must have faith. You must trust in me. You must believe that I wouldn't turn you loose if harm was going to come to you. You must believe that you will be safe, because I've told you that you will be." After a brief pause, he added, "Listen Toby, God holds you in the palm of His hand, and He always will, so long as you believe, so long as you have faith."

Toby began to protest. "Wait a minute. Faith! I don't know if I have faith or not? How will I know if I have faith! I think I'm gonna need some more time to think this over, this faith thing!" But by then Jesus had let go of his hand. Toby was frightened. The wind was howling, he couldn't see six inches in front of his face, and Jesus had let go of his hand. His fear began to overtake him, but he fought it. He thought about what Jesus had said. He knew that Jesus wouldn't just turn him loose and allow something bad to happen to him.

And suddenly he was struck by a thought—maybe Jesus had actually shown faith in him! Maybe Jesus showed his faith in Toby by letting him go. Jesus trusted Toby to obey his will, to keep moving forward no matter how afraid he was. As this thought settled in his mind he felt his strength and his resolve beginning to return. *Okay,* thought Toby, *if Jesus has that kind of faith in me, the least I can do is trust him, have faith in him . . . and believe what he said to me, no questions asked.* Suddenly Toby was no longer afraid. He did exactly as Jesus had said. He just put his head down and kept walking.

After what seemed like hours, Toby heard someone cry out. And even though the wind was howling fiercely, he recognized the voice. He'd know that voice anywhere. It was the gruff man, Peter. And Peter was calling out shakily, sounding like he'd seen a ghost. Toby was amazed that they had gone all the way around the lake so quickly and were already at the shore where Peter's boat would be. He looked through the grey, shimmering mist and saw Peter and the others in the boat. And then he saw Jesus standing near the boat. Some of the men thought that Jesus looked like a ghost and were afraid, but Jesus simply said, "Take courage. It is I. Don't be afraid." Toby looked over to where Jesus was, and he saw the strangest thing. Jesus was near the boat, but he wasn't on the shore—he was standing on top of the water! Just standing there, right on top of the sea!

Toby heard Peter say, "Lord, if it is you, tell me to come to you, on the water."

There was a brief pause. Then Toby heard a loud voice say, "Come," and he saw Peter lift himself out of the boat. And the next thing Toby knew Peter was walking on the water, walking right toward Jesus! Toby was amazed. But just then the wind really picked up and started howling and swirling. Peter became afraid, and when he became afraid he began sinking down into the sea, crying, "Lord, save me!" Jesus reached out to Peter and helped him back into the boat, saying, "You of little faith, why did you doubt?"

Peter and Jesus boarded the boat. Toby was watching, waiting to be told what to do. Jesus closed his eyes and turned his face up toward the heavens, praying. After a few moments he opened his eyes and the storm miraculously stopped. Just stopped. The wind stopped howling. The waves stopped thrashing. The sea became calm again, and as the clouds cleared away it gradually became lighter.

And then it happened. Toby looked at the boat, and it wasn't moored on the shore! It was sitting at anchor, right smack dab in the middle of the Sea of Galilee. The men had to set anchor in the middle of the lake because of the storm. The shoreline was just a distant sight!

Toby got the strangest feeling, and he slowly looked down. And when he did, he saw that he was not on the shore, either. He was standing right there on top of the water, just as Jesus had been! He was bewildered, and he started to get a little afraid, but then he heard Jesus quietly, but firmly, say, "Come." Toby figured maybe because he was so light he could do it.

He stiffened his resolve, lifted his head up, and walked right over to the boat. He climbed up and Peter helped him in. When the Disciples saw how Jesus had calmed the storm they began to cry, "Surely you are the Son of God!"

As the sailors set to work heading back to the shore, Jesus sat down in the back of the boat, and Toby sat down next to him. Peter was busy trimming the sails, and Andrew said something to him, calling him "the Rock." Toby looked up and said, "The Rock? What's that?" Jesus smiled and said, "His given name is Simon Peter. But I have given him a new name. I have named him 'the Rock.'"

Toby looked up at Jesus and said, "Why would you name him something like that?"

Jesus stared off into the distance and after a long pause he said, "Because he has faith, faith as solid as a rock . . . and upon that rock I will build my church."

Toby looked down and shook his head, saying, "Here we go with *faith*, again, huh? I'm really going to have to figure out just what this faith is all about."

Jesus smiled and said, "You saw Peter coming to me, did you not?"

Toby said, "I sure did. That was amazing!"

Then Jesus said, "Did you also see him begin to sink when he became scared and began to doubt?"

Toby said, "I did. I was afraid he would drown. But you saved him."

"Well, not exactly," said Jesus. "His faith faltered when he doubted, and he began to sink, but actually it was his faith that saved him."

Toby looked confused, and said, "If his faith faltered, how come it was his faith that saved him?"

Jesus smiled and said, "Well, Toby, sometimes when you're in doubt your faith can falter and you can feel yourself sinking. But God is always there. Always. He's always there to rescue you when you're in trouble. But you have to have faith that He will protect you, faith that He'll be there for you, faith that He'll rescue you. So, even though Peter was sinking, he cried out "Lord save me." It was his faith that led him to reach out to me, to believe that I would rescue him. So it was really his own faith that saved him—his faith in me."

Toby thought about this for a long moment, and finally said, "Wow, he's a pretty amazing guy, all right . . . 'the Rock.'" After a long pause he wistfully added, almost in a whisper, and really just to himself, "Boy, I'd give anything to be like him, to have that kind of faith."

Peter had overheard this conversation. He began laughing loudly and came over and stood beside Toby.

"What's so funny?" asked Toby.

Peter looked at him, his hands on his hips and shaking his head, and said, "You are, my little friend. You are."

Toby wasn't sure what to make of this. "What did I do that was so funny?" he asked.

Peter sat down and looked Toby right in the eye, and said, "You, my little friend—you who wants to know what faith is, you who wants to know if he has faith, you who are so envious of my faith—you just walked across half of the Sea of Galilee in complete darkness in the middle of a raging storm." He paused, and with a quizzical look on his face said, "Now, why on earth would you do such a thing?"

Toby shrugged and said, "I don't know . . . I did it because Jesus told me to. He wanted me to. And besides, he told me everything would be okay. He told me just to have a little . . ." Toby stopped dead in his tracks.

Peter said, "What is it, little friend?"

Toby's eyes welled up with tears, and he quietly said "Faith . . . Faith." He sniffled. "He told me just to have a little faith." Toby looked up at the big man and said, "I just did what Jesus told me to do, is all. I figured that if he trusted me to obey him, I should trust him, too."

Peter said, "Toby, when I became afraid I doubted, and I began to sink. But my faith in Jesus helped me overcome my fear and I relied on him to bring me in safely." He paused, then quietly but with great conviction said, "But you never doubted at all. Not once. Your faith never faltered. It never wavered. Oh, what I wouldn't give to have such a faith!"

"Wow," said Toby. "I never thought of it like that—faith, huh? Gosh," he mused, as much to himself as to Peter, "I suppose it was my faith in Jesus. But he also had faith in me. He knew I could do it, with his help. In fact, I think realizing that was what helped me to have faith."

Peter and Jesus spoke for a few moments, and then Peter went back to his work.

Looking out over the Sea of Galilee onto the distant shore Jesus quietly said, "Well, Toby, I guess you found it after all. You were always wondering if you'd know whether you had faith or not. I suppose now we've answered that question. And what a faith it is, my friend! Yours is a faith even 'the Rock' envies."

But Toby didn't say anything. In fact, Toby didn't hear a word Jesus said. As a gentle wind filled the sails and Peter's boat slowly turned toward the shore, in the silence all that could be heard was a tiny little sigh. Jesus looked down to find Toby on the deck of the boat wrapped in his blanket and clutching his little mezuzah, with the most contented, peaceful smile on his face, fast asleep.

Forgiveness

"Then Peter came to Jesus and asked 'Lord,
how many times shall I forgive my brother or
sister who sins against me? Up to seven times?'"
Matthew 18:21

THEY HAD BEEN BACK IN Jerusalem for a while, and as usual, Jesus began his days teaching in the Temple. Today Toby was sitting in the shade of a gnarled old olive tree waiting for him to finish. He had been thinking about all the people that Jesus had healed, so many that Toby had lost count. He had healed lepers, people with physical diseases, people with mental problems or possessed by demons, the blind, the deaf, the crippled, and on and on. And every time Jesus healed someone he would say, "Your sins are forgiven. Go forth and sin no more," or words very close to these. And right there, on the spot, these people were transformed. It was like they were made whole again, almost like they had been reborn.

Toby didn't really get it, even though he had seen it with his very own eyes. Not the healing part, that part he got. What he didn't get was how forgiveness had made such amazing changes in these people. He didn't get how Jesus could just say he forgave someone their sins and all of a sudden they would be whole again. Of all the strange and wondrous things Jesus did, this one baffled Toby the most.

There was good reason for Toby to be baffled by this. He had really struggled ever since losing his dad. The accident had left Toby with a great big empty hole inside of him. Unfortunately, that hole mostly got filled up with anger. He was angry at the man who caused the accident, and this anger spilled over into being angry at just about everyone. And though he didn't like to admit it, at times he even felt angry at God for letting such a thing happen. In Sunday School and church they always talked about God as being kind, gentle, and caring. Toby just didn't understand how such a God could allow something so terrible to happen to his dad.

And Toby wasn't always able to control this anger. A lot of times he had thought things, said things, and done things that ended up hurting others. A lot. Although he didn't want to admit it, underneath it all Toby had come to feel that he just wasn't a very good person. The notion of forgiveness never occurred to him. It never occurred to him to forgive others, and he just didn't believe that God would have much interest in forgiving someone like him. And truth be told, he wasn't sure that he had any interest in forgiving God, either. Besides, even if God were to forgive him, it was hard for Toby to believe that all the anger, hurt, and bad feelings inside of him would just disappear.

When Jesus finished teaching he came over to the tree, and Toby quickly pushed these thoughts aside. The pair made their way over to the home of the Widow Mary, where the others had already gathered for the mid-day meal. All day long Toby had been excited about seeing his friend John Mark again.

Toby was disappointed to learn that John Mark was at the Temple studying with the rabbis. And he was even more disappointed because with John Mark in the Temple, he would be the only one taking food upstairs to the men and cleaning up after they ate. He understood that this was part of what being a "helper" was, but he still hoped that this wasn't all there was to it. He stood by as the Widow Mary, Mary Magdalene, and the other women prepared the food, and then he took it upstairs.

When the men had finished their meal Toby began clearing the table. As was their custom after a meal, the men began discussing the events of recent days. As he often did, Jesus began to teach them about Heaven's Reign, and today he began teaching them about the nature of forgiveness. After some discussion, Peter turned to Jesus and asked, "Lord, please tell me, how many times shall I forgive my brother or sister who sins against me? Up to seven times?"

Toby thought *Hah! I wish Peter would have asked me that question. Seven times? Hah! I'd tell him not even once. No sir, not even once.* But as he headed down the stairs he heard Jesus say, "I tell you, not seven times, but seventy times seven."

What??? Toby was stunned. Hearing these words come out of Jesus' mouth stopped him in his tracks. He stood on the steps, suddenly flooded with all kinds of thoughts. He had never forgiven anyone in his whole life. It didn't make sense to him that you would just let somebody off the hook after they had done something to you. He very much preferred to spend his time plotting ways of getting back at them. At least that would give him some satisfaction, he thought. What good could forgiveness do you?

But hearing these words from the mouth of Jesus made him stop and think. Jesus always talked about how important it was to try to do God's will. Just like when he heard Jesus' sermon from the mountain that day, Toby began to realize that maybe his position wasn't so good after all. It occurred to him once again that his way of handling things may actually be going against God's will. Now, this was a scary thought. So scary, in fact, that Toby quickly tried to shake it off. Besides, he was still angry at God. If God was angry at him, too, well then maybe they were even. Underneath this bluster, though, the thought still scared him.

He was shuddering at these thoughts just as he entered the cooking area where Mary of Magdala was standing at a table cutting fruit. Toby looked up and saw that she had stopped what she was doing and was staring at him. He didn't know what to say—he was afraid she had somehow read his mind; that somehow she knew what he was thinking.

"What is it, little one?" she asked. Her tone still sounded kind and nice, so he figured maybe she hadn't read his thoughts after all. Whew!

"N-n-n-nothing," stuttered Toby. But he didn't make eye contact with her, just in case.

Mary continued looking at him, saying nothing. When Toby couldn't stand the silence any longer he fessed up, quietly saying, "I was just thinking about Jesus' teachings about forgiveness, and . . . and . . .", letting out a big sigh, he said, "well, I guess I just don't get it somehow."

Mary looked on him with great sympathy. She motioned him over to a little bench. She gathered him up into her arms and sat him on her lap.

"I'm going to tell you a story," she said. This was good. Toby liked stories. The smell of freshly baked bread and the comfort of Mary's lap brought him back to pleasant but very distant memories of his grandmother, and he just leaned back and relaxed.

Mary began. "Once upon a time there was a woman who was wracked by sin. She was a mess. Her life seemed empty and she felt dead inside. She was miserable, and it seemed like all the things she thought would make her happy backfired on her and just made her even more miserable. Around her town it was even said that she was possessed by seven demons."

Toby wasn't sure he liked where this story was headed.

Mary was quiet for a moment, and then with a little sigh, she said, "There came a time when this woman became physically ill. But she had been ill on the inside for a long, long time."

Mary paused and Toby saw a faraway look in her eyes. Then it dawned on him that this wasn't just some made-up story. This was a true story, and Mary was the woman. He began to feel sad for Mary. All of a sudden she looked at Toby as though seeing him for the first time. She held him tight and said, "But then something happened. One day this man, this rabbi, and his followers came through the woman's town. And as soon as she saw him she knew that there was something about this man, something very special. She had never seen anyone so kind, so gentle, or so compassionate in her entire life."

She paused, and then said, "And this man, he looked upon her with such compassion and pity! I don't know what he saw, but he must have seen something good in her, some goodness in her heart. Goodness that she had never been able to see. You see, she never would have thought that she was worthy of God's mercy and forgiveness. Especially when she couldn't even forgive herself."

She looked down at Toby, her eyes moist, and said, "But all of a sudden he just walked directly over to her. He looked deep into her eyes, and placed his hand on her head. And then in a calm, quiet voice he said, 'Daughter, your sins are forgiven. Rise now and be well.' And you know what? She did. And she was. He saved her. Right there on the spot. She had never felt so calm, so peaceful, in her entire life. And at that moment her life was turned around, like she had been reborn. It's been several years now, and she has been devoted to this man, this Jesus of Nazareth, ever since."

Toby felt a shiver go right through him. But just as he was about to say something, Jesus appeared in the doorway and said, "Toby, say goodbye to Mary. We need to hurry if we want to get up to the Garden before nightfall. The men have found shelter elsewhere, but I need to be up there this evening." As Toby headed out the door he turned and looked back at Mary, wanting desperately to say something to her. She smiled reassuringly and just nodded her head, and he could tell that he didn't have to say anything at all. Somehow Mary just knew.

They took the same short-cut they had taken the last time they went from the Widow Mary's home to the Garden of Gethsemane. To show that he obeyed Jesus' command to pay close attention, Toby asked if he could lead the way. They quickly made their way along the path, and soon they arrived at the clearing where the path wound deep into the olive grove. Toby recognized it instantly. There was a small clearing with several large rock formations on either side of the path that went back into the Garden.

Jesus stopped and said, "It's too open for you to sleep out here in the clearing, Toby. Just beyond those rocks on the far side you'll find a little thicket that's just your size. You can go on over and get some sleep. I need to spend some time back in the Garden alone with the Father."

Toby went directly to his little thicket, but he didn't sleep. He tried and tried, but sleep just wouldn't come. There were too many thoughts running through his mind. As he tossed and turned he thought about all the people whose sins Jesus had forgiven and Mary Magdalene's story and Peter's question and the things Jesus had said about forgiveness. And as he remembered these things, that nagging thought began to form in his mind again, and he began to feel afraid. He had come to the conclusion that maybe he'd been wrong to hold onto his anger the way he had. To hold grudges and never let anything go. Maybe he'd been wrong in never being willing to forgive anyone for anything. The more he thought the more he came to see that in fact he'd been a pretty rotten person much of the time. After this crushing revelation he didn't see how he could possibly deserve God's forgiveness. But then he remembered what Mary had said and was amazed that she had felt the same way. Could it be? . . . Could there be some chance that he, too, might be forgiven?

Toby was trying to sort out these thoughts when Jesus suddenly appeared. He had finished praying and had come to check on him. Jesus could see that something was bothering Toby. He led him out into the clearing and asked him what was on his mind.

Well, no way was Toby going to tell Jesus what was really on his mind. Not a word about how angry he was at the man or at God for what happened to his father. And he certainly wasn't going to tell Jesus his worst fear of all—that he had been so bad that he didn't even deserve God's forgiveness. After all, how could God forgive him after he had refused to forgive God? It was this fear that bothered him most of all.

As it turned out, though, once again Toby didn't have to say anything at all. Jesus had looked into his heart and already knew what was on Toby's mind. Toby looked up and saw an expression on Jesus' face. He had seen this expression countless times, only it had never been directed at him. When Jesus talked with people in great pain and in need of his healing touch, he didn't just sympathize with their pain—you could tell that he actually felt their pain. When he dealt with sinners, he actually took on his own shoulders the burden of their sin. You could see it in his face. And when he helped people who were in terrible anguish and turmoil—*ill on the inside*, as Mary Magdalene had put it—their pain became his own. Those were the times that Toby had seen that look, when people were wounded, broken, and in desperate need.

But this time was different. This time the look was aimed right at him! His heart sank. He could tell that Jesus had seen into his heart and was actually feeling the pain that he felt, and he began to cry. Soon he was sobbing uncontrollably. "Forgiveness!" he finally cried between sobs. "It makes no sense; I just don't get it." He looked at Jesus through his tears and said, "You forgive people their sins and tell them to go and sin no more, and they're made whole, right there on the spot. Just like that! I don't get it."

Jesus quietly said, "Toby, what you're seeing is God's grace. It's the awesome power of God's love, and their willingness to accept it, that makes them whole. Because of their faith they are able to trust in Him and to open their hearts to receive His grace."

But Toby was on a roll. "Not only that, but then you say that we're supposed to forgive other people. People who have hurt us, people who have done us wrong. On purpose! People who hate us, or who we hate. And we're supposed to forgive them *seventy times seven* times? I'm sorry, but I just don't get it!"

After a few moments of reflection Jesus looked at Toby and quietly said, "Toby, when I forgive people their sins I'm revealing something to them about God and God's grace. I'm revealing His love and important aspects of His nature. And one very important aspect is this: until you accept God's grace, until you accept that your sins are forgiven, you can't forgive others. It's only because you have received God's grace that you're able to truly forgive others."

Jesus continued, "God created man in His image. Because He loves us. And He wants us to show our love for Him by striving to be like Him. God's forgiveness is infinite, it's never-ending. That's what I meant by 'seventy times seven.' That's how much He will forgive you. And because He is willing to forgive you *seventy times seven*, He expects you to show that same forgiveness to your fellow man."

Toby seemed distant, lost in thought. "And He'll forgive anyone? Even people who are bad?"

"Anyone," said Jesus. "Anyone who opens their heart to accept His grace. He's always there. He always stands ready to forgive."

Then, in a small, small voice Toby asked, "Even me?"

Jesus said gently, "Toby, you can't hide from God. No matter how hard you try. And you've been trying pretty hard, my friend. But God knows what is in your heart. He knows how angry you are. He knows how much you hurt, and how much pain you're in. And His heart breaks for you."

"You mean He's not mad at me?" asked Toby.

Jesus laughed, and placed his hand on Toby's shoulder. "No, Toby," he said. "It's just not in God's nature to be angry with you. When people sin against Him, His heart breaks," said Jesus. "He feels sadness, not anger," Jesus paused, then said, "So then, the answer to your question, my friend, is 'yes.' God will forgive even you. Maybe even especially you."

After a moment, Jesus sat Toby down and said, "And you know what?"

"What?" asked Toby.

Jesus said, "I'm going to tell you a secret. And this is one secret you don't have to keep. The secret, Toby, is that He has already forgiven you."

Toby looked stunned and confused. "What?" he exclaimed.

Jesus calmly said, "That's the nature of God's grace, Toby. He knows your sins and He has already forgiven you. His grace is given freely, because that's how much He loves you. All you have to do is to open up your heart to receive it."

Toby wasn't sure he understood, but in the quiet stillness of the Garden he began to experience something strange. Something deeply emotional. Something from way down inside of him. Something he'd never felt before, ever.

Jesus just kept talking. "And when you receive His grace you'll be able to forgive others. Even *seventy times seven times*." Smiling, he added, "And that, my friend, is Heaven's Reign! That is God's will being done on earth just as it is in heaven. And the best part of all is that you will be the one doing it! You will be the agent of God's will right here on earth." He spread his arms once again and said, "Just open up your heart to receive His grace and you'll see. I promise."

The more Jesus talked the more flooded Toby became with thoughts about all the things that had been troubling him for so long.

He began to realize how these things had not only hurt him, but they had also hurt others. Especially his mom. When that thought struck him, Toby had no doubt about what had to be done. He had to let them go. He didn't understand exactly what Jesus meant by saying you just have to open your heart, but that didn't matter. He believed Jesus. He had faith in Jesus. He trusted Jesus as he had never trusted anyone in his whole life.

He closed his eyes, breathed deeply, and just thought about his faith in Jesus. And then he felt it. In that very moment, he could feel something begin to leave him. He could actually feel himself letting go. Letting go of the anger. Letting go of the hatred, the harsh feelings, the dark thoughts, all those things that had been part of him for so long. He began to feel lighter. A strange, new sensation was overtaking him. A feeling of warmth flowed through him. And within this warmth was a sense of well-being, a sense of safety, and above all, a sense of hope. And Toby suddenly realized what was happening. This is what Jesus was talking about! This feeling was God's grace washing over him. Freeing him. Cleansing him! He was feeling the power of God's love!

After what seemed like a very long time, Toby turned and slowly looked up at Jesus. There was so much he wanted to say, but he just couldn't find the words. Perhaps for the first time in his life, Toby was speechless, completely at a loss for words. But Jesus let him know that no words were needed. With a little smile he simply closed his eyes and nodded, and Toby could tell he understood. And for the first time in a very long time, Toby really *felt* understood. He turned and quietly made his way back to his little bed in the thicket. This time, though, he had no trouble at all going to sleep.

SECTION III

Trouble's Coming

CHAPTER 12

Lazarus—The Beginning of the End

> "Jesus called in a loud voice,
> 'Lazarus, come out!'"
>
> John 11:43

TOBY COULD BARELY CONTAIN HIS excitement when he saw the Jerusalem Gate and the house atop the hill. They had been staying away from Jerusalem, travelling in and around Galilee and across the Jordan River for quite some time, because the authorities down in Jerusalem wanted to do away with Jesus. But Jesus had received an urgent message from his good friends Mary and Martha. They begged him to come to their home in Bethany, just a mile or so beyond Jerusalem, because their brother Lazarus was ill. The Disciples were worried. They called Jerusalem the "killing zone" and begged Jesus not to go there.

The last time they were in Jerusalem there had been several attempts on Jesus' life which he barely escaped, and the Disciples were concerned for his safety. So they were relieved when Jesus didn't respond to the request. But then, several days later, Jesus all of a sudden decided to go. This puzzled them. They would have understood if he had left immediately to tend to his friend. And they even would have understood if he didn't go at all. But waiting three days, and then suddenly deciding to go? Well, this just didn't make sense. After a great deal of discussion and arguing, they decided to go with him, determined that if Jesus was to die, then they would die with him.

Even though Jesus was willing to put himself at risk by being seen in and around Jerusalem, he didn't want to put Toby in danger, so he instructed Peter to take him to the Widow Mary's home, where he was sure to be safe.

Peter carried Toby on his shoulders to save time, and by the time they had started up the hill John Mark was already running across the courtyard, shouting greetings to them. Peter slowed down and suddenly just shrugged Toby over his shoulders and placed him feet first on the ground. He told John Mark to take good care of Toby and turned to go. As he hurried away he called out over his shoulder telling John Mark to tell his mother to be sure to have one of those delicious fig pies for him when he returned. Roaring with laughter, he quickly disappeared down the road to Bethany to catch up to Jesus and the others.

As they ran to the house Toby could already detect the aroma of fresh baked bread wafting from the cooking area, and many comforting memories returned. John Mark said, "Well, Toby, this is a pleasant surprise. To what do we owe the pleasure?" Toby filled John Mark in on the events of the past few days and how Jesus and the Disciples were headed for Bethany. John Mark listened intently, and by the look in his eye Toby could tell he was up to something. "This must be important," he said. "Jesus is very close to Lazarus and his sisters—I wonder why he waited so long before going there?" Toby said, "I don't know. He said something about Lazarus' illness being for the glory of God, but I didn't know what he was talking about."

John Mark excitedly paced back and forth, hands clasped behind his back. "You know, Toby, I think this is big, this is big," he said. Then he suddenly stopped. "I'm supposed to spend the rest of the day in the Temple studying, but this is too big to miss." He thought a little more, and Toby knew what was coming. John Mark said, "Toby, I'd like for you to go to the Temple for me and talk to my rabbi. Tell him I won't be able to make it today, but I'll be there for sure tomorrow."

Toby had been to the Temple lots of times, but never all by himself. Seeing the look of concern on Toby's face, John Mark added, "If anyone says anything to you, just show them your mezuzah, and tell them you're staying with me, and everything will be okay." Then he said, "I'm heading over to Bethany. After the Temple you come back here and rest. You've had a long journey. I'll be back soon and fill you in on what's going on."

Toby still looked worried. "Relax," John Mark said. "I've done this a hundred times. I've got it down to an art. I'm quiet, I'm crafty, and I know just how to hide so I can see them but they can't see me!" He paused, then smiled. "How do you think I got so many stories, anyway? And I have a feeling this is going to be one of them!" he said, excitedly. "I'll tell you all about it when I return." John Mark scampered over to the terrace, climbed down his linen rope, and was out of sight before Toby could even make it out to the terrace. Toby's trip to the Temple was uneventful, and when he returned he went straight to John Mark's cot and sat down. Before he knew it he was fast asleep.

It was dark when Toby was abruptly awakened by John Mark, who was standing over him chattering excitedly and waving his arms around. "Wake up, Toby! Wake up!" he said. "You won't believe what happened in Bethany!" Toby sat up and started to say something, but by then John Mark was already out on the terrace. He was climbing down the rope and called back to Toby, saying, "Follow me!" Toby was only wearing a loin cloth, so on the way out he grabbed a white linen cloak from one of the baskets along the wall and put it on.

He climbed down the linen rope and ran over to the pomegranate trees. Before he could even get situated John Mark began talking excitedly. "I beat them to Bethany," he said. "Instead of following the road I took a short-cut I know, and I got to the home of Lazarus before Jesus and the others. There was a huge crowd of people gathered in the courtyard, wailing and beating their breasts, and I could tell they were in mourning. I asked a young woman what had happened, and she told me that Lazarus had died! He died several days ago, and they buried him just over the hill in a tomb carved out of a hillside." He took a deep breath and continued. "So I went over there, but just as I got there I spied Jesus and the others coming down the road. I found a good tree and climbed way up to the top of it, figuring I'd wait until they passed and then make my way back to the home of Lazarus."

He paused, and Toby said, "Okay, so what happened?"

"Well, as it turns out I didn't have to go to their house, because first Martha, and then Mary came running down the road to meet Jesus. They seemed kind of upset at first," he said. "They told Jesus that Lazarus had been dead for four days, and that he was already in the tomb. Each one said that if Jesus had been there sooner, Lazarus wouldn't have died."

"And . . .?" said Toby.

John Mark scratched his head, and said, "Well, when Martha said that, Jesus told her that Lazarus would rise again. Then he asked her if she believed in the resurrection. She said 'yes,' and then he said something, something you could never imagine in a million years."

Toby was getting impatient. "What?" he cried. "What did he say?"

John Mark said, "He said 'I am the resurrection and the life. The one who believes in me will live, even though they die, and whoever believes in me will never die.' Just like that."

"Is that it?" asked Toby.

"No, no," said John Mark. "Then Martha said, 'I believe you are the Messiah, the Son of God, who has come into the world,' and then Jesus looked at her and told her that she was right, that he was really the Messiah."

"Wow," said Toby quietly. He had never heard Jesus say that to anyone other than the Disciples. He looked at John Mark and, with a little worry in his voice, said, "What happened then?"

"Well," said John Mark, "he just said 'Where have they laid him?' and that was it. But when they led him over the rise and he saw the tomb, he changed. It looked like something stirred in him, some-thing moved him very deeply, and for the longest time he just stood there, not saying anything. And while he was just standing there a huge crowd gathered around. It looked like all of Bethany and half of Jerusalem had gathered out there on that road! They couldn't see it from the road, but from my perch in the tree I had a perfect view of the tomb," John Mark said. "After a while Jesus said, 'Take away the stone.' But Mary and Martha both argued with him. They said that Lazarus was four days in the tomb and that surely he must stink by now."

John Mark took another breath, and Toby said, "Boy, I bet he really did smell bad by then."

John Mark stopped him abruptly and excitedly said, "But get this! Jesus said, 'Did I not tell you that if you believe you will see the glory of God?' And then he told the men to remove the stone."

Toby was almost breathless. He said, "And what happened then? Did it really smell real bad?"

John Mark said, "Enough with the smelly stuff, okay? That's not the point. Anyway, I wasn't close enough to smell it. After they rolled away the stone Jesus spread his arms and looked up at the heavens, and then prayed, loud, like he wanted everyone around to hear him."

Toby said, "Well, what did he say?"

John Mark said, "He said 'Father, I thank you that you have heard me. I knew that you always hear me, but I said this for the benefit of the people standing here, that they may believe that you sent me.' I'll remember those words for the rest of my life."

"Why?" asked Toby.

"Because," said John Mark, "then he just stared at the tomb, and in a voice I've never heard before, real guttural and low, like it was coming from way down deep inside of him, he shouted, 'Lazarus, come forth.' Just like that! And his voice echoed off of the hillside."

"What do you mean?" cried Toby. "'Lazarus come forth,' what the heck does that mean? Lazarus was dead."

John Mark said, "I didn't know either, I had no idea what he was doing. But the next thing I knew I saw a shadow sort of move across the opening of the tomb. Then nothing. But then just a few moments later the shadow almost filled the whole opening of the tomb. And then, the next thing you know, here comes Lazarus, still wrapped in linens, walking right out of that tomb where he'd been dead for four days! Incredible!"

"Y-y-y-y-you mean," stammered Toby, "h-h-h-he actually raised Lazarus up from the dead?"

John Mark said, "He surely did, right there in front of Mary, Martha, most of the town of Bethany, and half of Jerusalem."

"In front of everybody. And he wanted everyone to hear his prayer, that he was revealing the glory of God!" Toby said, absent-mindedly shaking his head.

"What's the matter?" asked John Mark.

Toby looked deep in thought, and then said, "Well, he told Martha he was the Messiah. He thanked God for giving him the power over life and death, the power to raise Lazarus from the dead. In front of everyone!" Toby continued shaking his head. "In front of everyone! Don't you see? He did it so everyone would know he's the Messiah!"

John Mark laughed. "Well, of course they will! Do you just think he was showing off?"

Toby looked defeated. "No," he said. "You don't understand. It's just that now the people have seen his power. There's no denying it now. His enemies had already heard about him forgiving sins, which only God is allowed to do. But they didn't believe it was actually the power of God within Jesus that allowed him to do that. They accused him of blasphemy and said he was possessed by demons."

He kept on shaking his head. "But this, this thing that he just did, this leaves no room for doubt. He just revealed his absolute power over life and death. Demon-possessed men can't fake that one! No. Everyone knows only God has this power, and yet the whole town of Bethany and many from Jerusalem saw him bring Lazarus back from death! Boy! When this gets back to his enemies there's bound to be big trouble. They've already tried to kill him several times. But this time they have a real reason! He has claimed that he and God are one and the same!" Toby's voice suddenly got very soft. "There's just no turning back from here."

John Mark slapped himself in the head in anger, shouting, "You're right, Toby, you're exactly right! How could I not have seen it!"

Toby said, "Seen what? What do you mean, how could you not have seen it?"

John Mark said, "Well, it was getting dark, so I couldn't take the short-cut through the woods. I climbed down from the tree and ran along the road. And as I ran I came up to a whole big group of people. As I passed one group I heard them singing Jesus' praises and calling him the Messiah and thanking God that he was here to deliver them," He continued. "They were headed to Jerusalem to tell everyone the good news."

"At first I thought it was great. But then I passed a group of men who weren't happy at all. In fact, they were angry. They were accusing Jesus of all kinds of witchcraft, accusing him of blasphemy, and talking about how dangerous he was. Especially when the Romans see the kinds of crowds that will be following him now that he announced he's the Messiah. They were headed straight to the Temple to tell the elders what had happened."

Toby's heart sank. "Oh, boy," he whispered. "This could be it. Raising Lazarus may have set things in motion that we'll never be able to stop. This could be bad, John Mark, really bad."

Little did Toby know how true those words were. While he and John Mark were talking, people were already at the Temple telling the Pharisees and Temple Priests of Jesus' miracle and warning them about the huge number of new believers that would be drawn to Jesus because of it. Even as Toby was giving voice to his fears, Caiaphas, the High Priest and the most powerful man in the Temple, stood before the Pharisees and Temple Priests gathered around him and loudly pronounced a formal death sentence on this man, this Jesus.

CHAPTER 13

The Betrayal

"Then Satan entered Judas, called
Iscariot, one of the Twelve."

Luke 22:3

JESUS AND THE MEN DID not return from Bethany for quite
some time. Jesus had taken the Disciples out into the wilderness beyond the town. Although Toby missed them, it was okay
because at least he knew they were safe down there. But the time for
Passover, the highest of the Jewish High Holidays, was coming. Toby
had major concerns about what might happen if Jesus returned to
Jerusalem to observe Passover, as the Law compelled him to do.

Toby had gotten into a routine of helping the women with
cleaning, cooking, and laundry most mornings while John Mark was
at the Temple. He was a good helper, and he liked the fact that all
the women made such a fuss over him. He spent his afternoons playing or studying at the Temple with John Mark and discussing their
"stories." In the evenings when John Mark was studying, Toby spent
his time on the terrace, holding on to his mezuzah and thinking. He
enjoyed watching all kinds of different people come and go in and
out of Jerusalem through the city gates. He also spent a great deal of
time studying the lay of the land, memorizing various landmarks and
trying to picture different short-cuts in his mind's eye.

From his perch on the terrace he could tell exactly where the
Temple was, although he couldn't actually see it. He could tell exactly
where the road went past the home of Joseph of Arimathea. He could

also find Golgotha on a clear day. For reasons he didn't understand, this always made him shiver just a little bit. He knew the road to Bethany well, and could see the clearing where the short-cut began. He could also see Mount Olivet, and he pictured in his mind the short-cut up the back side to the Garden of Gethsemane. From the terrace Toby felt like he could feel the heartbeat of the city.

But things were different at night. People only traveled during the daylight, for fear of bandits and robbers along the road. And the townspeople were in their homes, typically asleep shortly after nightfall. In the evenings there was none of the hustle and bustle that he observed during the daytime. The desert sky was always clear, and there were no trees above the terrace blocking his view of the stars above.

The only thing that disturbed the peaceful dark and quiet of the night were the times when he could see the light from the torches of Roman soldiers as they made their way through the streets of Jerusalem. Seeing the Romans move at night was usually not a good sign. There was always some sort of unrest among the occupied Jews. There was a large group of rebellious men called Zealots who were determined to drive the Romans out of Palestine, and they often staged uprisings. But the Romans were equally determined to keep things quiet in Jerusalem. Pontius Pilate, the brutal Roman governor, thought that any uprising or disturbance would make him look bad in the eyes of his bosses back in Rome. So it wasn't unusual for the Roman soldiers to come through the city at night and roust people that they considered to be trouble-makers. They liked to arrest people at night rather than in the daytime, because there was less risk of townspeople forming a mob and causing trouble. Toby grew to both hate and fear the Romans, just like everyone else in Jerusalem.

One evening Toby was asleep on the terrace and was awakened by a very excited John Mark who was climbing up the rope to the terrace. He was completely out of breath, and Toby thought he looked terrible. "I've just come from Bethany," John Mark said breathlessly. "There's something big going on, but I couldn't stay."

"Why not?" asked Toby. "It's still pretty early."

"It's not that," said John Mark, still out of breath. "I think there's something wrong with me . . . I don't know what it is, but I think I'm sick."

"That would explain it," said Toby. "You look terrible and you can't seem to catch your breath—and I mean it, you really look terrible," he said with a frown. "What can I do to help you? Should I get your mom?"

"No," exclaimed John Mark. "She'd keep me in, and I believe there are some big things in the works. Just help me over to my cot and get me some water, if you would." Toby helped his friend over to the cot, but when he put his arm around John Mark's back to steady him he felt just how wet and clammy his skin was.

"Oh, boy," exclaimed Toby, "you don't just think you're sick, you really are sick! I think you've got quite a fever. You're burning up!"

He helped John Mark to lay down on his cot and asked him what all the excitement was about. John Mark said, "I was at the Temple today and I heard some men talking about a party at the home of a man in Bethany, a man called Simon the Leper." He gasped for air. "They said that Lazarus was sure to be there, and with Passover so near they also thought there was a good chance that Jesus and the others would be there, too. They thought they'd be coming through Bethany on their way back to Jerusalem for the Passover feast."

"Wow," exclaimed Toby, "it sure would be good to see them again. I've really missed them—but isn't it still dangerous?"

"I don't know . . . probably," said John Mark. "There will be at least a million people in Jerusalem for the High Holiday. Jesus and the others may be able to just slip into the city unnoticed. But even if they do, it'll still be dangerous. There's a warrant out for Jesus' arrest, and all the authorities are out to get him. If they get their hands on him they'll kill him for sure. In fact, the more I think about it, the more I think you're right, Toby, he will be in danger! They all will! We had better get down to Bethany and warn him!" But when he stood, all the color left his face and he began to wobble, as though he was about to fall.

Toby steadied him and helped him back down onto the cot and said, "Correction: maybe *I* had better get down to Bethany to warn him. You are surely too ill to travel, or do much else, for that matter."

John Mark frowned and began to talk. But his speech was very slow and quiet. "I don't know," he said. "I'm afraid maybe you're right . . . I'm really not in much shape to do anything . . . the best thing I can do is to rest up and get better . . . and then you and I can go there together."

"You're not going anywhere!" exclaimed Toby. "You're going to tell me what's going on and I'm going to be your eyes and ears until you're better. I'm going to go there and report back to you so you can write your stories."

"Well," said John Mark, "the party is scheduled for tomorrow in the late afternoon. I'll tell everyone that you're helping out at the Temple, helping to prepare for the Passover feast, and you can go see what's going on."

Toby said, "Okay, but in the meantime I'm going to get a wet cloth for you to put on your forehead and then I'm going to go and get your mom." When John Mark didn't respond, Toby looked closely at him and saw that he was already asleep. He went and got the Widow Mary who came and attended to John Mark, and Toby returned to his perch on the terrace.

But sleep wouldn't come. Toby tossed and turned for a very long time, his head swimming with all sorts of thoughts. He replayed the words that Jesus had said to others, words that began to take on an ominous tone. "I am the resurrection and the life . . . the Son of Man will be taken up . . . the one who believes in me will live, even though they die, and whoever believes in me will never die . . . the Son of Man is going to be delivered into the hands of men. They will kill him . . ." and on and on.

Toby would never tell John Mark this, but the truth was he was a little afraid. Since he had been there he hadn't had to do anything on his own. And he wasn't sure he could handle the Bethany situation all by himself. For all his bluster, Toby actually was a little lacking in the self-confidence department. He was a helper, but he didn't feel like he'd been much help. But what if this turned out to be important? What if this was the *Big One,* and what if he wasn't up to the task? What if this was his big chance and he blew it? The more he thought about this, the more unsure of himself he became. As his worry mounted, Toby laid flat on his back and tried to relax.

From the terrace he had a clear view of the night sky. As he looked up at the stars, he became mesmerized. In the clear, silent and cloudless night, he reflected on his conversations with Jesus atop the thinking rock up near Capernaum. And then all of a sudden it came to him: *Faith!* he said to himself. *That's it! It's all about faith. I have to have faith that Jesus will be okay and that God will give me the wisdom and strength to do what He needs me to do. I won't be down there alone, after all, I'll have God with me! I just have to have faith.* With this last statement still echoing in his thoughts, Toby fell into a deep, calm and restful sleep.

The following day Toby got up and helped the women just like every other morning. But in the afternoon he didn't go to the Temple. He made his way down to Bethany, taking the short-cut that John Mark had described to him.

As he neared Bethany he spied a home with lots of people, both inside and outside. He worked his way around the house and found a great spot where he could see and hear, but was still well hidden. He heard excited chatter about Lazarus, who had become quite a celebrity in Bethany since Jesus raised him from the dead. And then a woman ran out into the yard and announced that the rabbi was about to teach. When someone in the crowd asked who the rabbi was, the woman exclaimed, "Why Jesus, of course, the Galilean. Jesus of Nazareth!"

It was all Toby could do to keep from shouting out and rushing into the house. But he couldn't. If Jesus had wanted him to be there, he'd have told him to be there. So for now all Toby could do was watch and listen, and then report back to John Mark. It seemed so simple, Toby began to wonder why he had worried so much. But like so many things that seem simple, things got complicated real fast. Toby was in for quite an evening indeed.

By the time Toby got back to John Mark's home it was way past dark. Toby was exhausted, but also excited and dying to tell John Mark what had happened. He wearily climbed up onto the terrace and crossed the upper room, careful not to make a sound. When he first saw John Mark, Toby was shocked. His friend looked dead. He was pale and still, and his garments were soaked with perspiration. Toby knew that John Mark needed to rest, but this was too important to wait. "John Mark, John Mark, wake up," he whispered, gently shaking John Mark's shoulder.

John Mark stirred and slowly opened his eyes, and with the realization that it was Toby standing there, he shot bolt upright on his cot. "Toby, what is it?" he cried. "You look like you've seen a ghost!" Toby began jabbering excitedly, and John Mark finally said, "Calm down, Toby. Here, sit," and he patted the cot next to him. "Sit down, take a deep breath, and tell me your story," said John Mark calmly.

Toby took a few moments to gather himself. "Okay," he said. "But speaking of ghosts, you actually look like one! What in the world have you got?"

"Forget about me!" cried John Mark, "Just tell me the story!"

Toby said, "I was in Bethany at the home of Simon the Leper. Jesus and all the Disciples were there, and so was Lazarus, looking very much alive. Which is more than I can say for you, my friend."

"Gee, thanks," said John Mark, "but how about instead of a running commentary on my health, you just finish your story."

"Okay, okay," said Toby. "So they're all there, and everyone is happy, eating and talking and all—everyone except Judas, that is."

"Judas!" said John Mark. "He's the one from Iscariot, the one that keeps track of the money and all, right?"

"Right," said Toby, "and funny you should mention that, because Jesus was teaching, and there was a woman there who was sitting at his feet. In her hand she had this alabaster vial of some kind of perfumed oil. She let her hair down and poured the whole vial on the ends of her hair and used her hair like a mop to anoint Jesus' feet. Now, I didn't see anything wrong with it. In fact, I thought it was kind of a nice gesture. But not Judas! He got really mad. He seemed really bitter and angry, saying that they had wasted something that he could have sold for lots of money to give to the poor."

"Well, that's probably true," said John Mark. "If it's what I think it is, that stuff is precious and pretty expensive. But it's still kind of strange. It sounds like the stuff they use to anoint the body when someone dies."

"Well," said Toby, "Jesus didn't seem to be worried about that. He kind of got after Judas, saying something like 'leave her alone.' He said this out loud and in front of everyone else, and I think it embarrassed Judas. Then Jesus said, and I tried to memorize every word, so you can write them down: he said 'She has done a beautiful thing to me. The poor you will always have with you, and you can help them any time you want. But you will not always have me. She did what she could. She poured perfume on my body beforehand to prepare for my burial.'"

"Wow!" exclaimed John Mark. "So it really was the stuff they anoint dead bodies with! Plus, it sounds like Jesus knows something bad is coming, like he's prophesying his own death."

"You may be right," exclaimed Toby, "because at that very moment Judas changed. His face got all twisted up and for a second he looked just like Satan, or like in that moment Satan just overtook him or something! It was really scary! But it was only for a moment, and then it passed and Judas just turned and left the party."

"Well, if he was embarrassed that would make some sense, I guess," said John Mark.

"Way, way worse than that," said Toby, his voice trembling. "You don't know the half of it."

"Only because you're taking so long to get to it. Tell me! What is it?" said John Mark, sensing something big was afoot.

Toby said, "Well, I really wanted to stay at the party to tell Jesus and Peter and the rest to be careful, but something told me I'd better follow Judas and see what he was up to."

"Well done," said John Mark. "Go on."

"John Mark, he headed straight for Jerusalem, and when he passed through the city gate he made a beeline right for the Temple," said Toby. "He was being real sneaky, sticking close to the walls of the buildings he passed and constantly looking over his shoulder. I had to follow him from a good distance so he wouldn't see me, and I almost lost him a couple of times."

"The Temple," cried John Mark. "What on earth kind of business would he have at the Temple?"

"Nothing good," said Toby, "of that you can be sure. He was way ahead of me, so by the time I got to the Temple he was already there. I crossed into the Court of the Gentiles, and I couldn't see anyone, but I heard some people talking in hushed tones, like whispering. I couldn't tell what they were saying, though, because I was too far away. So, I crept along the wall until I got to the corner, and when I peeked around the corner I saw Judas, not ten feet away from me, and he was talking with three men who looked like Temple Priests."

"Temple Priests," cried John Mark, "why they're the enemy. They report directly to Caiaphas! They're the ones who are out to get Jesus! Them and the Romans! What on earth would he be doing with them?" John Mark wondered aloud, but even as he asked the question it was clear he had an idea of what the answer might be. He turned and stared at Toby in disbelief.

"I don't know," said Toby, "because I couldn't hear them, but I would be willing to bet that it's not good. They were all being real sneaky and talking like they didn't want anyone hearing what they were saying. All I heard for sure was something about the Passover feast, but I don't know what it was."

"This sounds really bad," said John Mark, but he said it almost absent-mindedly.

"And then," said Toby, "I heard something really odd, but I couldn't really tell what it was."

"Well, what did it sound like?" asked John Mark.

"You know, it sounded like tinkling or clinking, like coins, like in a money pouch or something," said Toby. "They could have been giving him money for something, but I really couldn't hear well enough to be sure."

"They're paying him for something," said John Mark. "I'd bet on it!" But the excitement of the moment had taken its toll on his strength, and he was fading fast. "But we probably don't have anything to worry about. Jesus may not even come to Jerusalem for the Passover . . . he knows full well how dangerous the city is . . . and even if he does come, there will be about a million people here . . .

he could just slip into the city and slip back out without anyone ever knowing." By the time John Mark finished this thought he was flat on his back again, and very soon he was snoring gently, fast asleep.

Toby wished that he was as certain about Jesus' safety as John Mark had been. He went to his sleeping place out on the terrace and spent the next few hours looking at the stars and going over and over the landmarks in and around Jerusalem in his mind. He didn't know why, but he felt certain that this would become very important, and very soon.

CHAPTER 14

The Triumphal Entry

"Say to Daughter Zion, 'See, your king comes
to you, gentle and riding on a donkey.'"
Matthew 21:5

TOBY CONTINUED TO SPEND HIS time doing chores, helping out around the house, and tending to John Mark, who was still quite sick. Just before mid-day he was out on the terrace resting when a low, rumbling sound got his attention. It was coming from the direction of Bethany, and it sounded like there was a crowd of people on the road singing or chanting or something. He kept his eyes on the crest of the hill, and soon he saw the strangest thing. There was a huge crowd of people moving toward Jerusalem. Some people were running ahead of the crowd laying palm fronds in the road. Some people were even laying their cloaks and tunics out in the road.

As the crowd grew nearer, he heard them chanting over and over:

Hosannah! Hosannah!
Blessed is he who comes in the name of the Lord!
Blessed is the coming kingdom of our father David!
Hosannah in the highest heaven!

And then in the midst of the crowd he saw this man riding a little donkey. Instantly he recognized the man as Jesus! Toby was surprised to see him, and mystified that he would enter the city in

such a way. Because Jesus' life was in danger in Jerusalem after raising Lazarus, he and the Disciples had been in the wilderness east of
Bethany for some time. Toby had missed them, but he consoled himself with the knowledge that they were safe down there. Seeing Jesus
headed to the city gates caused Toby to worry a bit, and he would
have awakened John Mark if he had not been so ill.

He and John Mark had debated whether Jesus would come to
Jerusalem for Passover. John Mark thought that Jesus and the others
might sneak in and out of the city under the cover of darkness, or
that Jesus would simply disguise himself and get lost among the hun-
dreds of thousands of pilgrims, Romans, Jews of Palestine, and various onlookers and curiosity seekers that would gather in Jerusalem
for the High Holiday. Toby was a bit more cautious, hoping that
Jesus and the men would just let this holiday pass on by without
coming into the city at all, even though Jewish Law demanded that
all able-bodied adult male Jews in Palestine attend.

Not in their wildest dreams would either of them have pre-
dicted the scene that Toby saw before him! In his studies with John
Mark, Toby had learned that the donkey, the palm fronds, and the
crowds chanting *Hosannah*! were all signs, part of a prophecy, a
prophecy that any Jew would almost instantly recognize. A prophecy
proclaiming nothing less than the long-awaited Messiah, the king of
the Jews, their deliverer and salvation. It was one thing to announce
his Messiahship to Mary and Martha and those gathered in Bethany
when he raised Lazarus. But this! This was different. Far from sneaking into the city under the cover of darkness, Jesus was boldly and
defiantly letting any and all in the city know his true identity—the
Messiah!—and on the eve of Passover at that!

Toby felt a mixture of excitement and concern. Jesus knew full well
there was a price on his head. Both the Jewish elders and the Roman
authorities were on the lookout for him. Entering the city in this manner
was certain to grab their attention, and not in a good way.

It was a very hot day with barely any breeze at all, and the sun
was high in the sky, directly overhead. Because of the heat, Toby had
been resting on the terrace wearing only his loincloth. He ran back
into the room and grabbed the first thing he could find, a long white

linen nightshirt. He threw it on, eager to get to Jesus as quickly as possible. He gave John Mark a quick once-over and then climbed down off the terrace and made his way down to the road as fast as he could. But by the time he got to the road, the crowd had passed through the gate into the city and was heading for the Temple. The crowd following behind Jesus was about twice the size of the crowd in front of him, and in the narrow streets of Jerusalem their movement slowed to a crawl. Toby couldn't get around the mob and he couldn't work his way through them. He knew that at this rate Jesus would reach the Temple at least an hour before he would, so he just relaxed and moved along slowly with the tempo of the crowd. He wasn't worried about finding Jesus. He would be preaching in Solomon's Porch, just like always. Knowing Jesus' courage, Toby also knew that Jesus would be there despite the obvious risks involved.

As they neared the Temple gate the street widened and opened up onto a vast cobblestone plaza, and the crowd quickly spread out and began to pick up speed. Two men were passing in the other direction, having just left the Temple, and one called out to a man walking near Toby. "Have you heard the news?" the man cried out.

"No," said the other man, and he moved away from the crowd to join the other two.

Well, this made Toby curious, so he moved in the same direction, just a few yards behind the man, to try to listen in on their conversation. "You should have seen it!" cried the first man, but before he could say anything else, the other man chimed in: "You know that Galilean, that Jesus fellow?"

"Yes," said the man. "I've heard him teach in the Temple before. He has quite a presence."

"Quite a presence, indeed," said the first man. "We were at the stalls waiting to get our money changed, and you know how it is during the High Holidays; there were people all around trying to sell maps, offering tours of the Temple for a fee, selling sacrificial doves, and hawking all sorts of souvenirs to people passing through into the Temple. It was just pandemonium through there."

"Yes," chimed in the other man. "And I look up and I see this Jesus fellow coming our way, toward the court. And he's got this look on his face like he's not happy with what's going on in there. And before you know it he's making a whip out of cords, and he starts thrashing the money-changers, overturning their tables, setting all the doves free, and driving everyone out of the Temple, the whole time shouting, 'Is it not written—My house will be called a house of prayer for all nations?—but you are making it a den of robbers.'"

"And," chimed in the first man, "he did all of this in front of the Temple authorities, the Pharisees, and the Temple Priests. Right under their noses! And they didn't do a thing—they just stood there. Afterward he went over to Solomon's Porch and just started teaching, like nothing had happened, just as calm and self-assured as always."

The other man said, "In the middle of his lesson a group of Pharisees came over and interrupted him and said: 'By what authority are you doing these things? And who gave you that authority?' But Jesus was too smart for them. He turned the tables on them and said, 'I'll ask you a question, and if you answer mine, I'll answer yours.' And then he asked them where John's baptism came from, did it come from heaven or from man?"

The first man excitedly jumped in, saying, "Do you see the trap he laid out for them? If they say it came from heaven, then he's going to skewer them for not believing in John, because Herod had John beheaded. On the other hand, if they say it came from man, they might just have a riot on their hands because many of us believe that John was a prophet."

"So what did they say?" asked the friend.

Both of the other men began laughing, and the first one said, "They got together and talked among themselves, and then turned to Jesus and just said 'We don't know.' And so Jesus says, 'Then neither will I tell you by what authority I am doing these things.' And he just turned his back on them and picked up right where he left off when they interrupted him."

Their friend began shaking his head back and forth, and said, "We'll have to see who has the last laugh. I'll bet that's not the last we'll hear from those Pharisees and the elders."

"You can bet on that!" said the first man, and the men said goodbye and went their separate ways.

CHAPTER 15

A Lesson in Love

"For God so loved the world that he gave his
one and only Son, that whoever believes in
him shall not perish but have eternal life."

John 3:16

BY THE TIME TOBY FINALLY made his way over to Solomon's Porch, Jesus had finished teaching. He smiled when he saw Toby walking toward him, saying, "Somehow I thought I might see you here today, my friend. My goodness, it's been a long time, have you grown?" Jesus slyly looked him over and said, "Oh, I'm sorry . . . did I wake you?"

Toby looked down and for the first time noticed he was wearing a nightshirt. His cheeks got red, and he was clearly embarrassed. He explained that in his hurry to get to Jesus he just grabbed the first garment he could find and threw it on. He was thrilled to see Jesus, but he noticed that Jesus looked weary and a bit pensive and pre-occupied. Toby said, "I'm so glad to see you. Gosh, it seems like it's been forever. I hope you can take some time to rest up, and maybe we could talk a bit at some point."

Jesus nodded wearily and said, "That's just what I was thinking, my friend. There are some things that I need to tell you. Let us go over to the Widow Mary's home and see about getting some lunch. Then maybe we can chat while we eat."

"Great idea," cried Toby, but before they had gone ten feet toward the gate Jesus was approached by a man. Toby could tell by the man's clothes that he was a scholar, a scribe, a very learned man. This man asked Jesus which of all the commandments was the greatest. Toby thought this was just another riddle, just another attempt to "trap" Jesus. But apparently Jesus had looked into the man's heart and saw that the request was in earnest, and so he replied, "The most important one, is this: 'Hear, O Israel: The Lord our God, the Lord is one.'" Toby recognized this from the Shema prayer inside of the mezuzah he wore around his neck. Jesus continued: "Love the Lord your God with all your heart and with all your soul and with all your mind and with all your strength. The second is this: 'Love your neighbor as yourself.' There is no commandment greater than these." The scholar agreed that these two commandments were greater than any others, and certainly more important than sacrifices or burnt offerings. As they turned to leave Jesus said to the man, "You are not far from the Kingdom of God."

When they got to the house they sat in the shade of the pomegranate trees out front, and Mary made them a lovely tray of bread and various fruits. It felt very peaceful to Toby. A cool breeze wafted down out of the hills around Jerusalem, cooling things off, the birds up in the trees were warbling, and the smell of ripe pomegranates was in the air. This, plus being with Jesus once again, filled Toby with a sense of peace. Toby began by filling Jesus in on some of the things that had been happening, but then stopped and said, "Jesus, I'm interested in what you told that scholar in the Temple, the thing about the greatest commandment of all. I've been studying a bit with John Mark's rabbi in the Temple, and I thought we had learned that no one commandment was any more important than any other, that they all are treated equally. Is that right?"

"You are correct, Toby," said Jesus, "that is the way it has always been—until now, that is."

"What's different now?" asked Toby.

"I am," said Jesus. "I am what is new. That was part of the Old Covenant. But there's a New Covenant. And I am that New Covenant. I am here to bring about a new and different relationship between mankind and the Father. In the Old Covenant God rewarded the Jews when they were observant and righteous, and punished them when they were sinful and wicked. Unfortunately, they were sinful and wicked a lot more than they were observant and righteous."

Jesus continued: "One of the ways they atone for their sins is to present him with a sacrifice. A pure, unblemished, and innocent lamb is sacrificed as an offering to the Father in atonement for their sins. This will be the centerpiece of our Passover observances at the Temple. But sacrificial offerings, just like many of the other rituals, seem to have lost their meaning over time. More often than not, the sacrifice is not accompanied by true atonement. They don't change and turn away from sin. In a lot of ways these sacrifices and other rituals have just become a way to try and duck God's wrath rather than a means of actually strengthening the relationship with Him. The Father desperately wants to shower mankind with His love and mercy. He wants a relationship characterized not by endless rituals and animal sacrifices, but by love. That's it, pure and simple. Love."

"So that's what you meant in the Temple, the commandments about love," said Toby.

"Yes," said Jesus. "All the rest, the Law, the Prophets, and everything else rests upon this commandment. If you love the Father with all of your heart, mind, and soul, and love your fellow man as I have loved you, everything else takes care of itself." He was silent for a time, and looked weary and pensive. Toby started to tell Jesus about Judas, but Jesus just waved him off, as though he already knew what Toby was going to say.

"Toby," he said, looking the boy directly in the eye, "you must have faith. And trust that all things are in the Father's hands. He works in many strange and mysterious ways to implement His will. We may not understand why He does many of the things He does, but we have to trust in Him always, no matter what." Toby didn't quite know what to make of this, so he just silently nodded.

Jesus added, "Things are beginning to happen very fast. A lot of things are going to happen over the next few days that you probably won't be able to fully understand. Some may even seem cruel and cause you to wonder if He's really in charge at all. So, I wanted to talk with you a bit so that you will be prepared for them when they happen."

Toby remained silent (always a tough thing for him to do). But he had learned that if he didn't pepper Jesus with question after question, Jesus would eventually tell him everything he needed to know. So he waited silently. After several moments Jesus said, "Toby, do you remember the times that I have said that it was not yet my hour?"

All of a sudden Toby couldn't find any words. He was scared by where he thought this might be heading. All he could manage was a little nod.

"Well, now my hour is near," Jesus said. "Very near, in fact. Soon the forces of evil in this world will have their day, and I will be delivered over to them."

Toby had heard Jesus tell the Disciples a number of times that soon he will be turned over to the authorities to be killed, but he never really thought that such a thing would actually happen. When the full reality of what Jesus was saying finally hit him, he was stunned. He felt like he couldn't breathe, like he was paralyzed. He wanted to shout out "No!" He wanted to argue with Jesus, to tell him he must be wrong! He wanted to plot with him ways to keep this awful thing from happening!

But he could tell from the look on Jesus' face that the time for such rantings had passed. He just kept quiet, a profound sadness washing over him. He simply shook his head slowly in disbelief and said, "You're right. I don't understand."

Jesus clearly could feel Toby's sadness. He said, "A vital part of my mission has been to reveal to people the nature of the Father and to show them how His will can be accomplished here on earth just as it is in heaven. I have spent a great deal of time teaching the Disciples about the Kingdom of Heaven. Together with other instruments of the Father's will, helpers, people like you, Toby, they will be able to carry this message out to the farthest corners of the world."

Toby said, "I hope the other helpers will do more to help than I have. I don't feel like I've been very helpful at all."

"Patience, my friend, patience," Jesus said. "You have no idea how valuable your contributions might be. Don't sell yourself short. Remember when you thought all you had to offer was two loaves and a couple of fishes?"

Toby laughed and said, "Okay, okay, I get it. I'll try to be patient." And then they both fell silent.

After a long pause Jesus said, "But teaching people about the Kingdom of Heaven is just one part of my mission. The other vital part of my mission here is to offer myself up as a sacrifice, just like the lamb at Passover. The will of the Father is that I sacrifice my life in order to atone for the sins of mankind. This, too, is a sign of God's love."

Toby could be silent no longer. "But why?" he protested. "It just doesn't make sense that He would show His love that way."

"Often, my friend, love involves sacrifice," Jesus said. "Toby," he asked, "have you ever been hurt badly?"

"Yes," said Toby. "One time I fell out of a tree and broke my arm really bad, and I had to be in the hospital for surgery on it."

Jesus said, "I'm sorry; it must have hurt terribly."

Toby said, "You bet it did; it hurt really bad."

"Well," said Jesus, "do you suppose that your mom might have been willing to take that pain on herself in order to spare you from it?"

"Sure," said Toby. "In fact, she even said so, she said she wished it was her instead of me. And she would have done it, too."

"I don't doubt that for a moment," said Jesus. "Because she loves you."

Toby seemed deep in thought, very deep. He quietly said, "And you know, sometimes when I see her crying or missing my dad really badly I have wished that I could take his place so she wouldn't have to be so sad."

"And I'm certain she has also had thoughts that she would trade her life if it meant you could have your dad back," said Jesus. After a brief silence Jesus added, "And that is the essence of love, my friend, that is the very essence of love."

Toby thought a little more, and finally said, "But I thought God was merciful. Why would He let such a thing happen? Especially to you! How could that possibly be a sign of His love?" protested Toby. "That just makes no sense!"

"Because," said Jesus patiently, "God is indeed a merciful God, but He is also a just God. There is a debt that is owed because of mankind's sinfulness. Justice demands that the debt be paid. And the debt is so huge that nothing short of my own sacrifice can clear it."

As Jesus was talking, Toby began to "connect the dots" in the events of the past several weeks—the raising of Lazarus, the rebuke of Judas and the defense of the woman who anointed his feet with the perfume. All of his statements prophesying what would happen to him. And the triumphal, defiant entry into Jerusalem, topped off by cleansing the Temple right in front of the authorities. The very authorities who were out to kill him.

All of these events, everything that had happened over the past few weeks, they were all pointing to one terrible, awful outcome. Suddenly Toby felt sick, and very heavy, like he was glued to his chair, unable to move. It was like his brain was moving in slow motion. All he could think of to say was, "I am so sorry, Jesus."

Jesus smiled and said, "Thank you, Toby." After a brief pause he said: "But just as there is a time for sorrow, there is also a time for joy. You're just focusing on the sorrowful part right now. Of course, evil will have its day, and it will be brutal and ugly, because sin is brutal and ugly, and I will be sacrificed in the process. And evil will rejoice, believing that this is a great victory over everything that is good. But Toby, listen carefully: No one is going to take my life from me. I will give it over freely, of my own free will. This is the cup that the Father has given to me, and I intend to drink from it freely. The Father also loves the world. In fact, He so loves the world that He gave His one and only son, so that whoever believes in him, even though he dies, shall not perish, but shall have eternal life in union with Him in Paradise. He will resurrect me and return me to Paradise to be with Him, and also to prepare a place for you and all other believers. And that's the joyous part."

"Through my sacrifice the atonement will be complete and through my resurrection He will overcome evil and demonstrate His absolute power over death and evil to the entire world. My sacrifice is the ransom for man's sinfulness. It is the ransom that saves you from sin, the ransom that guarantees you forgiveness through God's grace, and the ransom that purchases everlasting life on your behalf. The resurrection will break death's hold on mankind and ensure that all believers will rest with Him in Paradise—forever! After I'm resurrected and ascend into heaven I will no longer be with you in body, but I will be with you in spirit." Jesus then smiled and said: "So always remember, Toby, wherever two or more people gather in my name, I will be there with them. Right there with them. Until the end of time. I hope that you will find comfort in that, for that's the joyous part."

With that, Jesus rose to leave to find some solitude and commune with the Father prior to sundown, which was just a few hours away. As he walked away he looked over his shoulder and then, almost as an afterthought, he came back and knelt in front of Toby's chair. He said, "Toby, do you remember what you said when I told you that in my Father's mansion there are many rooms, and I am going go to prepare a place for you, for you and all believers."

Toby perked up a little bit on hearing this. "Yes," he replied.

"And do you remember what you asked me?" said Jesus.

Toby quickly said, "I asked if you really meant all believers," he said, with growing excitement, "and you said 'All believers, every single one.'"

Jesus said, "You do remember. And what did you ask next?"

The words had barely escaped Jesus' mouth when Toby excitedly shouted, "I asked if that included my dad! And you said 'Absolutely!' You said it absolutely includes my dad!"

Jesus said, "And that's the joyous part, too. Never forget that." He then rose, and as he walked away he said, "I am with you always, Toby, lo, even until the end of the world."

Toby was still pondering these thoughts as Jesus passed out of sight. He sat in the shade of the pomegranate trees and once again became aware of the gentle breeze and the sweet smell of the ripe pomegranates. He closed his eyes and breathed deeply, determined to savor this peaceful moment. He knew this was apt to be the last such peaceful moment for some time to come.

On some level he also knew that this had been a special moment with Jesus, and he focused on preserving the memory, for he knew somehow that this was likely the last such moment. Then he rose and quietly made his way up to check on John Mark and to his terrace to rest.

CHAPTER 16

The Longest Night

"'Truly I tell you,' Jesus answered, 'today—
yes, tonight—before the rooster crows twice
you yourself will disown me three times.'"

Mark 14:30

J OHN MARK HAD TAKEN A turn for the worse. The Widow Mary
had asked Peter to speak to Jesus, in hopes that Jesus would heal
John Mark. She was surprised when shortly thereafter Jesus came
to her directly and asked her to step out into the rear courtyard with
him. Jesus took her hand in his and with great compassion said,
"Mary, many things happen for the glory of God, to serve as revelations to others about His kingdom. You must do what you can
to help John Mark and leave the rest to your faith." He smiled at
her reassuringly, then quietly turned and left. Although she did not
completely understand, she accepted what Jesus had said and immediately sent for a physician, who came to the house and administered
a number of herbal remedies to John Mark. Afterward John Mark
spent the bulk of his time sleeping, punctuated by brief episodes
during which he was awake but delirious. On the few occasions when
he was awake and actually coherent, Toby tried to fill him in on the
events of the past few days, providing more and more material for
his stories.

Jesus had gathered the Disciples together in the upper room
to speak with them about a number of things prior to the Passover
meal. But before he addressed them he removed his tunic, and with-

out saying a word he began to wash their feet. Well, they were totally shocked! And a little disturbed. The washing of someone else's feet was a task performed only by slaves or servants (or children, as Toby had learned), certainly not one to be performed by the Messiah, the Son of God!

But Jesus did this for a specific reason. This was a revelation, demonstrating an important feature of the Kingdom of Heaven— menial service to one's fellow man. He explained that there is joy and fulfillment to be found in humility and service to others, and he encouraged all the men to follow his example after he was gone. He also spoke to them at length about the things that he had told Toby in the courtyard earlier in the day.

As the time for the meal drew nearer, more and more people arrived at the Widow Mary's home, and it got a little crowded in the upper room. The Disciples were there, along with all the Marys and a number of other friends and followers of Jesus. With John Mark still under the weather, the job of helping the women serve the meal and waiting on the guests fell to Toby. Although it was a lot of work, Toby enjoyed it. Passover was a very important religious observance, but it was not a somber one. It was a celebration, a celebration of the time when God spared the Jews from the Angel of Death as Moses was demanding that Pharaoh free his people from bondage. So there was lots of eating and drinking, singing, chanting, and all sorts of good cheer. And boy, was it noisy up there! So noisy that people had to shout in order to be heard much of the time.

On one of Toby's trips upstairs he heard Jesus say to the Disciples that one of them would betray him. Toby stopped and listened closely, hoping to hear who the traitor was. He was sure it was Judas, of course. But the men at the table didn't accuse anyone. Instead, each man seemed to be worrying that he might be the betrayer. Toby remembered when Jesus had waved him off this afternoon, and now he understood it was because Jesus already knew what Judas had done. Keeping these thoughts to himself, Toby just kept on working.

As the eating slowed down, Toby finally had a chance to sit and relax a bit. As was his custom, he took his place directly behind Jesus on the floor. This evening Jesus was sitting at the head of the table, with John the "Beloved Disciple" to his right and Judas Iscariot to his left. Amid all the noise and bustle, Toby noticed that Judas Iscariot was scowling, looking very unhappy as he turned and said something to Jesus. With all the commotion, Toby was the only one who seemed to notice this. He decided to sneak in a little closer and listen in to their conversation. Just as he got within earshot he heard Jesus say to Judas, sadly, and almost in a whisper, "What you are about to do, do quickly." And Judas immediately got up and left, his departure unnoticed by the crowd.

Toby was about to go and wake up John Mark and tell him about this, but all of a sudden things got quiet, and Jesus stood up to talk. He looked around the room, then held up a loaf of bread and said a prayer. Then he said that the bread represents his body, which was given over for our sins. He broke off pieces of the loaf and passed them to the Disciples, saying, "Do this in remembrance of me." Then he did the same thing with the wine, saying it represents his blood, which was poured out for us. Then he had the Disciples drink from the chalice, saying, "Do this in remembrance of me." He led the Disciples in a hymn, and then said, "Let us depart for the Garden of Gethsemane."

Toby had been worried that Jesus and the men would be going into the city and to the Temple this night, which would have placed them all in great danger. He was relieved to hear they were going to spend the evening in the Garden of Gethsemane, away from the city. He could finally relax, and maybe get some sleep tonight. He helped the women clean up from the meal and looked in on his sleeping friend briefly before grabbing a couple of blankets and heading out to the terrace to finally get some sleep. He looked down at his tunic and saw that it was filthy, after undergoing numerous trips up and down the stairs carrying food and drink, and always in a hurry. He shed the tunic and put it in the hamper for soiled garments, then took a long white linen nightshirt out of the clean hamper. It felt clean and crisp. He went out onto the terrace in the twilight, prayed for the safety of those he loved, and fell right to sleep.

As much as Toby had looked forward to a good night's sleep, a long night of restful sleep would not be his. Not on this night. He had only been asleep for about two hours when he was awakened by loud voices below on the road. He looked in the direction of the voices and saw a group of at least twenty Roman soldiers headed toward the city gate, illuminated by the torches they were carrying. One of the soldiers had turned and called out to another group of soldiers a ways down the road, telling them to hurry.

Toby knew right away that something was afoot. It was not at all unusual to see lots of Roman soldiers inside the city gates, especially during the High Holidays when Jerusalem was crowded with people. But these soldiers were not from the garrison in the city. They were coming from the south where there was a small garrison of Roman soldiers who guarded the aqueduct that brought water into the city. *With over a thousand Roman soldiers already in Jerusalem, what would the authorities need with these men?* Toby wondered.

The first group of soldiers stopped at the city gate and were talking while they waited for the others to catch up. Toby was dying to hear what they were saying, so he rushed off the terrace wearing nothing but his white nightshirt. He didn't even stop to put on his sandals. He crept up to the hillside overlooking the gate and listened. The soldier he had heard shouting was obviously in charge and was giving his men instructions. Toby heard him say, "We were called away without any warning. There was no time for me to be fully briefed on our mission. All I know at this point is that Pilate commanded us to meet up with Caiaphas' guards at the gate."

One of the soldiers said, "Caiaphas? He's the High Priest of the Temple! What business do we have working with Temple guards?"

"I'm not sure," replied the leader. "It seems that Caiaphas requested Pilate's assistance in taking care of a sensitive situation. All of Pilate's men are tied up keeping order in the city, and he couldn't spare any to aid Caiaphas, so he sent for fifty of us."

Another soldier said, "You know how these Jews are. They're always stirring up trouble of some sort. Maybe they need reinforcements to put down some type of rebellion."

The captain said, "I don't think so, and besides, they already have a thousand soldiers—what good would a mere fifty more do them? No, this is some type of operation for the benefit of Caiaphas, something so sensitive that the Jews are afraid to undertake without a Roman presence. I think the messenger said they want to arrest someone, or take someone into custody, but they want to do it quietly and discreetly, so they don't start a riot."

Then it hit Toby. The gate! The gate! They weren't talking about the city gate. They were standing at the city gate, for goodness' sake. The only other gate it could possibly be was the gate to Mount Olivet! To the Garden of Gethsemane!

CHAPTER 17

Faith, Hope, and Love

"A young man, wearing nothing but a linen
garment, was following Jesus. When they seized
him, he fled naked, leaving his garment behind."
Mark 14:51-52

HE HAD TO WARN JESUS! Toby scrambled down through the courtyard, but just as he got to the road the other group of men were right in front of him. He crouched behind some shrub in the ditch beside the road and held his breath as the group passed by. The moon was full and there were no clouds to block its light. Toby was afraid that his white nightshirt would stand out in the light of the torches, but the men were busy talking to each other and not paying any attention to their surroundings. They passed right by him. Although he was out of their torchlight, he knew he still had to contend with the moonlight, but he couldn't wait any longer. He scuttled across the road and headed up the back side of Mount Olivet, up the short-cut to the Garden of Gethsemane. Toby had visualized the trail to the Garden so many times that he knew it by heart. He was moving fast, determined to beat the soldiers to the Garden.

He was breathless when he reached the point where the trail leveled off, so he stopped to catch his breath. He knew he was near the Garden, so he began to move slowly and quietly. As he emerged from a little thicket on the trail he could see Jesus and the others in the moonlight, standing right at the entrance to the Garden. Jesus was saying something to the men, but with the wind rustling through the leaves Toby could barely hear him. He moved in a little closer and sat completely still, holding his breath.

He heard Jesus say, "You shall all be offended because of me this night. You will all fall away, for it is written 'I will smite the shepherd and the sheep shall be scattered.'" This seemed to strike fear in the Disciples, but then Jesus added, "But after I am risen I will go before you into Galilee." Jesus' words also struck fear in Toby, because he made the connection of Jesus being the shepherd and the Disciples being the sheep that would be scattered!

While he was still pondering the meaning of this, Toby heard Jesus tell Peter, James, and John to come with him to keep watch while he went into the Garden to pray, while the rest were to wait for him up the trail where there was a cave that would give them shelter. Toby had to backtrack and go around the back side of the Garden to avoid being seen. He found his familiar sleeping place, a little thicket right by a large clearing. But by the time he got there he could only see the three Disciples in the clearing. He figured that Jesus had gone deeper into the Garden, as was his custom, to pray. Toby looked again and was shocked to see that the three men were all sleeping. Jesus had said to keep watch, but they were sleeping!

Toby thought he should probably wake them, but just then he heard Jesus approaching. When Jesus emerged from the darkness, Toby was struck by the sorrowful look on his face. When Jesus saw that his three Disciples were sleeping, his face showed even greater sadness. He said, "Peter, are you asleep? Couldn't you keep watch for just one hour?" Peter stirred, groggy and drowsy, and Jesus said, "Watch and pray so that you don't fall prey to temptation. The spirit is willing, but the flesh is weak."

He then went far back into the Garden once again, and was back there for some time. When he felt it was safe, Toby thought he would go and talk to the men to see what he could do to help, but when he peeked out from behind the thicket he saw that the three men were asleep again! He was confused and a bit overwhelmed by all that was happening. He didn't know whether to wake the Disciples, to run back into the Garden and warn Jesus about the soldiers, or to go and wait with the others. None of these seemed like a good option, so he just stayed glued to his spot and tried to hear what Jesus was saying back there.

The wind was rustling the leaves on the fig trees, so he couldn't hear much. He decided to creep past the sleeping men so he could hear what Jesus was saying. Just as he got past the first dense cluster of olive trees he heard Jesus say, "Abba, Father, all things are possible unto Thee; if it be possible, take this cup from me." Toby froze. After a long pause, Toby then heard him say, "Nevertheless, not what I will, but Thy will be done". Jesus was asking God to spare him, to deliver him from his fate!

Toby was stunned. So stunned, in fact that he almost didn't notice that Jesus had finished praying. He scampered back out of the Garden and once again took up his place behind the thicket. And he was just in time! Just as he cleared the thicket he saw Jesus step into the clearing. The three Disciples were still sleeping. Jesus roused them, and spoke to them, but their eyes were very heavy and they didn't know how to answer him.

He sadly turned and walked back into the inner recesses of the Garden. Seeing Jesus in this state filled Toby with an overwhelming sadness. He didn't see how Jesus' situation could be worse. His friend and comrade Judas had betrayed him. His three most trusted and loved Disciples had fallen asleep right when he needed them most. And worst of all, it sounded like despite Jesus' pleas he was not receiving any answer from the Father.

Toby's heart was breaking for Jesus. He felt a compelling urge to rush back into the Garden and let Jesus know that there was at least one person who hadn't abandoned him! One who hadn't betrayed him! But just then Jesus emerged again from the Garden. This time, though, he looked different. He still looked sad and sorrowful, for sure. But he had a look of determination on his face. It was obvious—he had reached a decision. *This could be great!* thought Toby. *Maybe the Father actually took the cup from him and spared him from a horrible fate! How great would that be?* But just when Toby began to think that maybe God had delivered Jesus from his fate, his hopes were dashed. And just when he had thought Jesus' situation couldn't get any worse, it got worse. Jesus came over and awakened the three men and sadly said, "It is enough; the hour has come. Behold—the Son of Man is betrayed into the hands of sinners." And they headed back to join the others.

This is it, thought Toby. *The hour has really come.* Quaking with fear, he quickly made his way back to where he had first spied Jesus and the men. He saw them gathered there again, but they were just standing there, looking down the hill toward the gate. Toby moved down the hill closer to the road to get a better look, and crouched behind a bush. He gazed at the road going down the hill and instantly froze. There must have been over a hundred people moving through the darkness carrying torches! Among them were the very same soldiers he had seen at the city gate, and they were all carrying swords. And others in the mob were carrying big clubs. And then Toby's heart sank. He spied Judas—Judas! The Betrayer! Judas was at the head of the procession, right in front! Leading the mob right up to Jesus! When they came into the clearing, the soldiers and Temple guards stopped. Toby saw Judas walk up to Jesus and kiss him on the cheek, supposedly a gesture of friendship. Jesus said, loud enough for all to hear, "Judas, comrade, you betray me with a kiss?" and all of a sudden the soldiers and Temple guards seized Jesus. Toby realized that the kiss wasn't a sign of friendship at all—it was a signal to the mob so they would know which man was Jesus. When they seized Jesus, Peter took up his sword and injured one of the soldiers. He was ready to fight to the death, but Jesus stopped him, saying, "Put the sword away—for all who draw the sword will die by the sword." Toby didn't know if they were aware of it, but Jesus had just saved Peter's and the other Disciples' lives, for the mob surely would have killed them straightaway.

Toby was amazed at Jesus' courage. Not only did he prevent a savage attack on his Disciples and save their lives, but he also seemed to take charge of the situation. He questioned the soldiers and Temple guards and made them look silly. He said, "Am I leading a rebellion, that you have come out with swords and clubs to capture me?" Then he showed what cowards they were by saying, "Every day I was with you, teaching in the Temple courts, and you did not arrest me." Then he said that the Scriptures must be fulfilled. He told the leaders of the mob that he was the one they wanted, and now that they had him in custody, they could let the others go, for they had done nothing wrong. The lead soldier thought for a moment, and then told the Disciples they could go.

The men immediately deserted Jesus, scattering in all directions. One of them ran very near to where Toby was hiding, and spooked a nest of rabbits. A large rabbit ran right at Toby, and he instinctively jumped backward, letting out a gasp. Suddenly realizing that he was exposed, he looked up and saw a Roman centurion staring right at him. The centurion shouted, "Captain, there's a boy up there!" The captain shouted back, "Seize him! Seize him!"

Toby just stood there frozen, staring at the soldier who had spotted him. He was so paralyzed by fear that he didn't see the other soldier until it was almost too late. He saw some movement out of the corner of his eye and turned just in time to see this huge soldier, who was bigger and angrier looking than anyone he'd ever seen, in mid-air, heading straight for him! In that instant time stood still. Toby felt glued to the spot, unable to move.

But at the very last second, he came to his senses and bolted right out of the thicket, running just as fast as his little legs could carry him, just as the soldier landed in the very spot that he was occupying just one second ago. The soldier had reached with all his might to grab Toby as he hit the ground, but Toby was too fast for him. The soldier missed Toby, but he managed to grasp the hem of the linen nightshirt. Well, Toby kept going, but the nightshirt didn't, and Toby ended up running all the way home naked.

Naked, perhaps, but also alive and well, and incredibly relieved. He made his way across the road and was sneaking up the hill in the moonlight toward the house when he heard a great commotion coming from the downstairs. He wanted to go over and tell them what had happened, but he'd be in big trouble for sneaking away and putting himself in such danger.

And besides, he was naked. He decided he needed to clothe himself before he did anything. He climbed up the rope and slowly peered over the ledge to see if anyone was there on the terrace. The coast was clear, so he climbed onto the terrace and tip-toed over to the outside wall of the house. He inched his way along the wall to the doorway and slowly stuck his head around the corner to risk a quick peek into the upper room. Seeing no one, he rushed in and grabbed a new nightshirt and slipped it over his head. Next, he went over to check on John Mark. He was desperate to let him know what had happened, but he couldn't seem to rouse him. It was only then that the noise coming from downstairs registered: people shouting, wailing, crying, moaning, and making the worst kind of noises! He saw the shadow of someone moving up the stairs, and quickly ran back out to the terrace and pretended to be asleep. He opened one eye just a little to peek at whoever it was, and saw Mary of Magdala appear in the doorway. She looked terrible, and there were tears streaming down her face. "Wake up, Toby, wake up!" she cried. "They've taken our Lord. They've arrested him and taken him away . . . I don't know what we're going to do!"

Toby rubbed his eyes and pretended to be waking up, but he was suddenly overcome by sadness. He looked at Mary's face, and he began to feel her pain and anguish. Not knowing what to do, but remembering how comforted he was that time when she had picked him up and put her arms around him, he went over to her and without saying anything just put his arms around her in a big long hug. He didn't know about her, but it made him feel a lot better, as the events of the evening began to sink in. Mary stopped sobbing after a time, but she was still distraught. She kept repeating over and over, almost in a whisper, "What are we going to do? What are we going to do?"

Toby walked her back downstairs, where people were attending to the Widow Mary. One of the women told Toby that the Widow Mary was already terribly worried and upset about John Mark's condition, and then she received news of Jesus' arrest. Upon hearing this, she just completely collapsed. Toby told the women not to worry, that he would sit with John Mark through the night and tend to him so the Widow Mary could get some rest, adding that he would call them if John Mark needed them. The women thanked Toby profusely and gave him a basin of clean water and a towel he could use to soothe John Mark. He left the mourning women and headed back upstairs. Even though he was dead tired, the only thing on his mind was shepherding his friend safely through the night.

Although in many ways his world was crumbling around him, Toby noticed that for some reason he actually felt calm. Almost serene, you might say. As he daubed the towel in the clean, cool water and placed it on John Mark's forehead, a number of disconnected thoughts ran through his head, things that Jesus had talked about in his teaching or in their discussions atop the "thinking rock"—compassion . . . empathy . . . self-sacrifice . . . menial service to others . . . and on and on.

Slowly, these thoughts began to come together, and Toby realized their meaning—love. These things were the love that Jesus had talked about! He thought about the fact that without even thinking about it, he had felt empathy with Mary in her sadness and had shown her great compassion in being there for her and comforting her with a hug. And how he so easily placed his concern for his friend above his own fatigue and need for sleep. And how he was willing to stay up all night tending to his friend, performing menial service for someone else, without even giving it a second thought. And again, he thought about how, despite the fact that the world seemed to be crumbling around him, he was calm. He slowly came to realize that this was because he had faith. He was calm and secure in the belief that everything rests in God's hands, and that even if things looked horrible from his perspective, from God's perspective everything was under control. And this gave him hope. *Faith, hope, and love,* thought Toby. *Go figure.*

This was God's love. And without even realizing it, Toby was showing God's love here on earth, just as it must be in heaven. Funny, though. He didn't feel proud of himself. He didn't feel the need to run up to other people and brag about knowing God's love. He didn't even feel like jumping up and down and shouting to the rooftops that he *got it.* What he did feel, though, was a very calm, serene inner peace and sense of well-being that he now understood what could only be described as joy.

Shrouded in God's love and with joy in his heart, he spent the remainder of the night tending to his friend.

SECTION IV

Trouble's Here

CHAPTER 18

The Longest Day—Morning

"Then Peter remembered the word Jesus
had spoken to him, 'Before the rooster
crows twice you will disown me three times.'
And he broke down and wept."

Mark 14:72

IT WAS JUST BEFORE DAWN that Salome, mother of John, the "Beloved Disciple," came up the stairs. The house had been quiet for most of the night, so quiet that Toby could hear the wind rustling the leaves on the trees out by the terrace. There was a rhythm to the wind that he found comforting, a reassurance that despite their troubles, God was still active and in charge.

He greeted Salome and asked her how things were downstairs. She said the Widow Mary went to sleep shortly after Toby had gone upstairs, so the other women had a chance to sleep as well. She said she was well rested, and now it was time for Toby to rest. Toby told her that John Mark mostly had a quiet night, but there were times when he cried out or seemed to be talking in his sleep.

"That's just the delirium," said Salome. "He'll be better soon, good as new, just you wait and see."

Toby said, "I sure hope so, and the sooner the better. I've been worried about him."

"We have, too," said Salome, "but he's resting well and the physician's remedies are working, so it should just be a day or two. Now off with you, you need to get some rest."

Toby didn't have to be told twice. He headed straight out to the terrace and went right to sleep.

Just after daybreak the women downstairs were awakened from their sleep by a loud knocking on the door. After the events of the night before, they were convinced that Roman soldiers were at the door, come to arrest them all. It wasn't until John cried out, "It's me, John! Son of Salome, and I have Peter with me! Please hurry!" that they dared to open the door. The Widow Mary opened the door and found John standing there, dirty and disheveled. He had his arm around Peter's back, just barely struggling against the big man's weight. Peter's eyes were open, but they just stared straight ahead, expressionless.

Mary gasped when she saw the two men and said, "My heavens! What has happened to the two of you? And what in the world is wrong with Peter?"

"He's in a daze, has been for quite some time," John said, adding, "he's had a tough night." He continued: "I'm sure you heard of Jesus' arrest last night."

"We did," Mary of Magdala said, "to our everlasting sorrow. Where have they taken him?"

"I don't know," said John. "We all scattered after Jesus was arrested. We thought we were doomed, but Jesus had such courage! After they seized him, he commanded the attention of the soldiers and Temple guards, and said 'You have the one you have come for. These men have done no wrong. Release them and let them be on their way.' And they did! We were all so amazed and frightened that we just ran and ran, in every direction."

"You abandoned our Lord?" cried Mary of Magdala, incredulous, and a bit angry. "Cowards! How could you have done such a thing?"

John became a bit defensive at this: "Of what use would we be to him in prison?" he said. "I caught up with Peter on the mountainside, and on the way down we ran into Phillip. He was planning to go down to Bethany, to the home of Mary and Martha, where the rest had gone to hide." John began shaking his head. "God forgive me, I wanted to go there, too. But Peter would have none of it. He was determined to stay as close to our Lord as possible until they released him."

One of the women arose from the cot she had been on and John walked Peter over and set him down on it. The woman lifted Peter's feet onto the cot, and he laid back breathing deeply, as though asleep, except that his eyes remained open, just staring blankly up at the ceiling.

"So we followed the arrest party, down the mountain and through the city. They took our Lord first to the home of Caiaphas, the High Priest, and then to the home of Annas, his father-in-law and the former High Priest."

"Caiaphas!" said Mary of Magdala, "He's hated Jesus from the beginning! He's been behind this all along! I guess he finally got his way!"

John continued: "Earlier in the evening Peter had let his pride get the better of him when Jesus prophesied what was going to happen to him. Peter denied Jesus' prophecy, and stated that he would die before he would allow such a fate to befall our Lord."

"What did Jesus say to him?" asked the women.

"He could see that Peter had given in to his foolish pride. He immediately rebuked Peter. Then he said not only would Peter not lay down his life for Jesus this night, but in fact he would deny ever knowing Jesus at all. He said that Peter would deny him no less than three times before the rooster crowed."

"Why, Peter would never do such a thing!" cried Mary of Magdala.

"I would agree with you," said John, "if I hadn't seen and heard it for myself. We settled in the courtyard to wait until they released Jesus. While we were there we noticed a lot of men were entering the home of the High Priest, and they were all members of the Sanhedrin, the high court! At first we thought they were going to put Jesus on trial for some charge or another, but we remembered it is unlawful to try someone at night—all trials must be carried out in the light of day, according to the Law. As the men filed in, we also noticed that neither Nicodemus nor Joseph of Arimathea was among them. This was very curious, since they are two of the most highly respected members of the Council."

Mary said, "Very curious that they would call a meeting of the Sanhedrin and not invite those two men in particular, since they are both also friends of our Lord."

"Curious indeed," agreed John. "We were in this little alcove, away from the fires in the courtyard, afraid that if we were recognized we would be arrested, too," continued John. "A servant girl who was on duty came by and saw Peter. She looked him over and asked him if he knew Jesus of Nazareth."

"And what did Peter say?" asked Mary.

"To my amazement, he said, 'No, I do not!' just like that. The servant girl stared at him for what seemed like an eternity, and then walked away. I asked Peter why he would say such a thing, but he just stared blankly and said nothing. After a time, we moved closer to the fires to warm ourselves. Peter asked a man if he would mind if we sat with him by his fire. But the woman next to him heard Peter speak and said, 'You have the accent of someone from Nazareth—surely you must know the Nazarene they have arrested.'"

"And?" said Mary.

"Again Peter denied knowing Jesus, denied ever even hearing of him," said John quietly. "A short time after that another man came by the fire, one of Caiaphas' men," he continued. "He stopped and looked at Peter for a long time, and then said, 'I know you! I have seen you with that Galilean, Jesus of Nazareth, haven't I? What business do you have here?'" John sat down, and then with great sadness in his voice said, "But Peter denied him again, a third time, just as our Lord had prophesied. And at that very moment the rooster crowed! Peter broke down and wept and let out this low moan, sounding like he had been mortally wounded." John motioned over to Peter laying on the cot as still as can be, just staring out blankly, and said, "and he's been like that ever since."

"I wanted to bring him here for you to tend to him," John continued, "but I didn't have the strength to support his weight this far. We were not too far from the home of Joseph of Arimathea, so we went there, and it was all I could do to get him that far."

"I hope no one saw you," said Mary. "It would cause Joseph a great deal of trouble if they were to see him with followers of Jesus."

John assured Mary: "I was very careful to stay in the shadows close to the buildings. And we didn't actually go to his house. We went around to the servant's cottage. We spoke to the servant and had him seek out Joseph for us. Joseph came out to meet us. We told him what we witnessed at the home of the High Priest, and he became quite upset and agitated. He had his servant bring us here to you, and I believe he went straightaway to the home of the High Priest."

Two of the women attended to Peter, and the others took John out to a courtyard near the cooking area. There they cleaned him up and brought him a clean tunic and washed his feet. They were about to fix him a large plate of fresh pomegranates, figs, bread, and olives, but he fell asleep before they could prepare it. When he awakened a little while later they brought him his meal and he crossed the courtyard to sit in the cool shade of a pomegranate tree. He had barely begun to eat when he heard a noise. Looking up, he was shocked to see Peter standing in the entryway, looking like his old self again. John's first impulse was to ask Peter what in the world had gotten into him last night, but he saw that *Don't even go there!* look on Peter's face and held his tongue.

Peter lumbered out into the courtyard and sat down beside John. Without a word, he took John's plate and just started eating. And eating. He had eaten all the bread, most of John's figs and he'd just started in on the pomegranate before he said anything. He looked out across the yard at nothing in particular and said, "There's a battle being waged inside me, my friend . . . and it came to a head last night. That's what you witnessed—I was paralyzed by it."

He looked up to the heavens and sighed. "You know, John, all my life I've had to rely on myself, on my own strength, my own wits, my own courage. I suppose at times I can be a bit of a blowhard, but that just comes with the territory. The point is, I take pride in these things, because I feel like they have made me who I am today. I'm proud of my strength, my courage, and my independence," he added, "But . . ."

"But what?" asked John.

"But then I met this man, this Galilean, like me. Except this Galilean is not like me. He is the Messiah, the Son of the Living God! And this man tells me not to rely on myself, but to trust in God. Not to be proud of these things, but to confess my weaknesses before the Father. Not to fight, as is my inclination, but to lay down my sword and seek peace. And not to be so consumed with false pride." And then, in a very small voice for such a big man, Peter said, "And I know he's right. Accepting him as my Messiah means I have to change, John, and it's hard. I have to forget about my own selfish will and seek to do his. I have to give up being angry, which I always saw as a source of my strength and power, and learn to be meek. I have to stop always trying to be first, and learn that it is okay to be last. I have to repay evil with kindness, hatred with love, anger with joy. Why, I have to become a totally new man . . . and it's hard, John, it's really hard."

"Gosh," replied John, a touch of sarcasm in his voice, "it's almost like you have to be reborn, to be born again in Jesus, the Christ," a sly smile lighting up his face.

Peter was stunned. He closed his eyes, crinkled his brow, and then slapped himself on the forehead and said, "So that's what he means! How could I have been so dense? That's exactly what he meant when he told Nicodemus a man must be born again in order to follow him! How could I have been so blind, John?"

John said, "We're all blind to one degree or another, Peter. But remember, my friend, you are still the Rock. When Jesus asks you to stop relying on your own strength, he wants you to stop relying only on your own strength. He's asking you to also rely on a greater strength as well. When he asks you not to place all your faith in yourself, he's asking you to place your faith in someone greater." John then became very serious. "Peter, you must understand you are our Rock as well. Like it or not, you are our leader. And there are mighty things we will need to accomplish. I see bad days ahead for us. The forces of evil are having their day with Jesus right now, but they're not just coming after our Lord. They'll be coming after us as well. All of us. And we will need you. We will need your strength, your courage, your leadership, your cunning, and your fighting spirit.

And I believe when you place your trust and faith completely in the Father, through Jesus, you will find strength, courage, and vision like you never imagined. We're counting on that, on you, to shepherd us through these very difficult times and to sustain us when we begin our work."

"That's a sobering thought, my friend," said Peter, "a very sobering thought indeed, and not one to be taken lightly." After several moments of silent reflection he stood, stretched out his arms and said, with great conviction, "But I'm your man! You can count on me, John. You can depend on me one hundred percent. For I am the Rock!" And then he quietly, almost sheepishly added, "Me and the Father, mind you, me and the Father. For the Father will be *my* 'Rock.'"

"Well done!" laughed John, "Well done!" And the two friends headed back into the house to get some rest.

Toby had missed all the action. He'd been sleeping soundly out on the terrace in the shade of the big olive tree, sleeping so soundly, in fact, that the commotion surrounding the arrival of John and Peter did not even cause him to stir. But there was no escaping the next sounds he heard. These were the sounds that would signal him that the whole world had changed. And that nothing would ever, ever, be the same again.

CHAPTER 19

The Longest Day—Afternoon

"Carrying his own cross, he went out to
the place of the skull (which in Aramaic
is called Golgotha). There they crucified him, and with him two others—one
on each side and Jesus in the middle."

John 19:17-18

TOBY HAD COMPLETELY GIVEN HIMSELF over to sleep, and slept through the night and into the next afternoon. But he was startled out of this sleep by the loudest wailing, moaning, and weeping he had ever heard. His first thought was that something terrible had happened to John Mark. He shot off the terrace, shed his blankets, and rushed over to John Mark's cot. But his friend was just as quiet and still as could be, and his breathing was deep and steady. Toby was relieved, the wailing, weeping and moaning having nothing to do with John Mark.

Seeing that his friend was all right, Toby's next thought was that the Roman soldiers were here to take them all away. He streaked across the upper room and flew down the stairs. When he reached the bottom, he saw Mary of Magdala, Salome, Mary, mother of James, two neighbor women, and a woman who looked vaguely familiar, but who he had never seen before. He would later learn that she was Mary, mother of Jesus. They were all holding onto each other as if for dear life, trembling, crying, moaning, and wailing inconsolably. John heard the commotion and came in from the back courtyard, saying,

"Ladies! Ladies!" somewhat impatiently. But when he saw the looks on the women's faces, he knew something was terribly wrong, and he spoke to them with great compassion.

Toby saw Peter coming into the house, trailing behind John, and quickly went over to his side. "What's all the commotion, friend?" Peter asked, placing a hand on Toby's shoulder.

"I don't know," Toby replied, "I've been asleep . . . but I'm scared, Peter, I think something's terribly wrong."

Peter said, "Well let's just go over there and find out," and he guided Toby over to where the ladies were standing.

Peter saw Mary, the mother of Jesus, sobbing, and immediately rushed over to her and held her in his arms. "Mary," he said, "I'm so sorry Jesus has been arrested. We'll do our best to get him back where he belongs. With you!" But Mary just sobbed and trembled even harder.

Salome, John's mother, said, "John, Mary and her friend ran into a man named Simon, from the village of Cyrene, on the way over here. He told them that the Romans have taken Jesus to Golgotha to crucify him! The Romans scourged him and then paraded him through the city on the way to Golgotha. He stumbled and fell, and that man, Simon, said he reached down and carried Jesus' cross for him until the Romans stopped him."

With that the weeping, moaning, and wailing started up all over again. John himself almost collapsed. He put his face in his hands and quietly sobbed. Toby felt like someone had stabbed him in his heart. He, too, began to cry. Afraid his legs would give out on him, he leaned against the wall and just slid down it until he was on the floor. Peter sat next to him and placed a reassuring hand on Toby's shoulder. After a few moments, Jesus' mother gathered herself together, dried her face, straightened out her tunic, and with great courage and determination, said, "Enough of this! I need to be with my son at his hour! I need to go to Golgotha right now. Mary, John, Salome, and Widow Mary, come with me! I need to be with my son!"

Toby ran over to John and said, in the best grown-up voice he could muster, "I'm going, too, John, I need to be with Jesus at his hour as well."

John turned and sternly said, "No, Toby, Golgotha is no place for a young boy to be, and the last thing on earth you need to witness is the horror of crucifixion. You do not wish to be scarred by witnessing the brutality they will visit upon our Lord. No, young man, you will stay here with Peter and tend to John Mark. That's how you can best serve our Lord at his hour."

Toby started to protest, but one look at the expression on John's face and he knew the man was serious. Dead serious. Although he was terribly disappointed, Toby was also kind of relieved. John was right—Toby did not want to witness the crucifixion or see the horrors that would befall his friend, Jesus. He turned and went up the stairs, determined to serve Jesus by tending to John Mark in the best way possible. After all, he reminded himself, no job is too small or menial in service of God's will.

Toby sat with John Mark, who was still sleeping and occasionally delirious, but the stress of the past twenty-four hours had taken its toll on him. He was completely exhausted and emotionally drained, and almost paralyzed by a profound sadness mixed with terrible fear. Suddenly, he felt like he was suffocating. The room seemed to get smaller and smaller, closing in around him, and the air inside the room felt stifling. He staggered out to the terrace just to get a breath of fresh air. He took a few deep breaths and then sat down with his back against the wall. But the instant he sat down, it felt like someone had just let all the air out of him. He quickly slid into a restless, fitful sleep.

As he tossed and turned he heard Jesus' words echoing in his thoughts: "I lay down my life—only to take it up again . . . on the third day he will be raised to life! . . . the Messiah will suffer and rise from the dead on the third day . . . the Son of Man must be delivered over to the hands of sinners, be crucified and on the third day be raised again . . . wherever two or more of you gather in my name, I will be there with you . . . lo, until the end of time." Then a new thought began to repeat itself in his mind, over and over and over: "After I have risen I will go ahead of you into Galilee . . . After I have risen up I will go ahead of you . . . Risen . . . Galilee . . . Risen . . . Galilee."

But these thoughts came to an abrupt halt when Toby was rudely awakened by a violent shuddering of the earth. It felt like an earthquake! And when he opened his eyes the world was dark all around him. At first he thought he might have slept the entire day and into the night, but this was a different kind of darkness. It was a quiet, still, cold, eerie darkness. Last night there was a full moon. But now there was no moon at all, and no stars in the sky. It was as though the entire cosmos had gone dark. Like God had simply turned out the lights.

Toby was frightened. He wanted to get inside and check on John Mark to make sure he was safe. He wanted to get away from the shaking and into the safety of the house. He knew he would feel safe and secure with Peter and the others downstairs. But he couldn't see! Even on the darkest of nights he could always see shadows or find some light to make his way back into the house. But not on this night. This night felt like the earth had died. He just stayed as still as he could and waited . . .

Within a few minutes the earth stopped shaking and the darkness began to lift. Light slowly crept back into the sky above him. As it became lighter and lighter, Toby realized it wasn't nighttime at all! It was the middle of the day! He reckoned the time to be about three o'clock in the afternoon by the position of the sun. As the darkness cleared and the shuddering stopped, Toby also felt the cool, comforting feeling of a gentle breeze. Hearing the rustling leaves of the big old olive tree again gave him a comfortable feeling and a sense that things were finally back to normal.

He went in to check on John Mark, who stirred a little, and opened his eyes. "Toby," he said, casually, "how are you doing?"

Toby had been waiting for this moment for almost three days! In his excitement he sat right down beside his friend and just started to rattle off everything that had happened since John Mark had fallen ill. But his friend quietly placed a hand on Toby's arm in midstream and simply said, "Water." Toby was embarrassed. "Why, of course you're thirsty," he said as he went over to the cistern and filled the cup. "I'm sorry, I don't know what I was thinking." John Mark thanked him and drank it down, then asked for more. As Toby went to the cistern he started again to fill John Mark in on the events of the past three days, but when he returned to the cot his friend was once again fast asleep, breathing slow, deep, and steady. Toby smiled, both at his own foolishness and at the happy prospect of John Mark's recovery. And then he heard it again.

From downstairs he once again heard terrible weeping, wailing, and moaning. These cries, wails, and moans were worse than before. These noises had an air of desperation about them, an air of panic and grief. In between wails he heard the voice of Peter, and then he heard John speaking as well. He hurried downstairs to see them. But what a scene he saw when he got to the bottom of the stairs! All of those who had gone to Golgotha were there, along with Peter and John and the two women from next door, and somewhere between ten and fifteen neighbors, all crowded in the little front room. The women were shaking and trembling, and all holding on to each other, with Mary, Jesus' mother, in the center being supported by the whole bunch. The women were completely distraught, and Peter and John looked lost, sad and bewildered. As Toby surveyed the group he began to put two and two together: the darkness that fell over the earth, the earth shaking as though it was dying, the eerie stillness that felt like God had simply left . . .

Jesus was dead.

Toby's knees became weak and shaky, his vision blurred, and he felt a terrible sickness that went right through him. His heart was aching as though someone had stabbed him. He began sobbing as he shakily sat down on the bottom step, his head in his hands. The Widow Mary, her eyes puffy and red and her face swollen from so much crying, moved past Toby as though in a daze, and made her way up the stairs to check on John Mark. He looked up and saw John and Peter sitting on the floor over by the door. John was sobbing, with his face in his hands. Peter, who looked stunned and broken, had his arm around the Disciple, trying to comfort him. Toby moved over toward them, and as he approached, Peter looked up, and without saying a word he simply lifted his other arm, an invitation to Toby to join the two men. Toby sat down with Peter's arm around him and buried his face in Peter's cloak and just sobbed and sobbed.

CHAPTER 20

They Have Killed Our Lord

"Some women were watching from a distance.
Among them were Mary Magdalene, Mary the
mother of James the younger and of Joseph,
and Salome." "Mary Magdalene and Mary the
Mother of Joseph saw where he was laid."

Mark 15:40,47

ONE OF THE NEIGHBOR WOMEN had been in the back for quite
some time, and she returned with a platter of freshly baked bread,
ripe figs and pomegranates, olives, and some assorted nuts. Her
friend followed behind her, carrying a jug of wine and enough glasses
for everyone, even Toby.

Mary, Jesus' mother, wiped her face, straightened out her tunic,
and with a look of determination and courage she broke away from
the other women, once again taking charge of the situation. She
moved over to the stairs, walked up three of them, and then turned
to face the group. Everyone fell quiet. All that could be heard was the
wind rustling gently outside, the chatter of some birds up in the big
olive tree, and the occasional sniffle. Mary looked around the room
from face to face, with the same look of compassion and pity that
Toby had seen on Jesus' face so many times. Then, in a voice that was
quiet and calm, but strong nonetheless, she simply said, "They have
killed our Lord." At this a number of the others began crying once
again, but Mary quieted them down, saying, "There will be plenty

of time for sorrow. For now, we have things to take care of, for the Sabbath draws near."

One of the women said, "What have they done with our Lord, my lady?"

Mary said, "We left that horrible place once my son lost consciousness. We all know the kinds of things the Romans do to complete the work of crucifixion, and I could not stay and see my son treated that way. I asked John and the others to bring me back here." She then said, "I want you to know, though, that your Lord not only showed great courage throughout his ordeal, but in spite of what they had done to him, through his actions he also revealed to us the face of God." She paused, steeling herself. "After they nailed him to the cross and the first wave of agony had passed, Jesus looked down at the Roman soldiers who had crucified him. He looked into their hearts with compassion and love. Then he turned his face toward the heavens and said, 'Father forgive them; for they know not what they do.'"

"Two lowly criminals were also crucified at the same time, one on each side. One of them chided Jesus for forgiving the Romans. But the other defended Jesus, and then said, 'Remember me when you come into your kingdom.' Despite his pain and suffering, Jesus reached out to the man and reclaimed his soul, saying to his defender, 'Truly I tell you, this day you will be with me in Paradise.' And later, just before he lost consciousness, so near death, he still placed the needs of others ahead of his own agony and suffering. He looked down on me from the cross with great sadness, and said, 'Mother,' and then shifted his gaze to John and said, 'behold your son.'"

John interrupted at that point, saying, "Yes, and then he looked at me and said 'Son, behold your mother.' This was his command that after he was gone the care of his mother would be entrusted to me. Even in the throes of death, he was still concerned for Mary's well-being in his absence."

Mary then proudly said, "Let that be a lesson to us all. Jesus did not just talk about grace, mercy, and forgiveness—he lived it. He *was* God's grace, mercy, and forgiveness. Even after all that was done to him he continued to do the Father's will here on earth, just as it is done in Heaven." She went on: "His brothers James and Jude will be coming for me shortly, but afterward I will remain with John, the Disciple that Jesus so loved." She smiled a sad smile and said, "To his everlasting glory in God's eyes, Joseph of Arimathea had the courage to petition Pilate to have my son removed from the cross and be placed in his custody so that Jesus could be buried properly according to our Law. There was some urgency to his request, as sundown is approaching, and as you know our burial rituals can take quite a bit of time."

"What did that monster Pilate say?" asked another woman.

"He agreed, but only after making sure that Jesus had given up the ghost," she said courageously, obviously holding back tears. "He dispatched his centurion, Cornelius, to Golgotha to certify that my son was dead. Cornelius then assisted Joseph and Nicodemus in delivering the body to Joseph's garden, where he will be laid to rest in a tomb Joseph had carved out of a little hillside there. Joseph had the tomb made for himself," said Mary proudly, "but he gave it over to my son."

After a rather long silence she wistfully said, "It is truly a beautiful garden where my son will be laid," almost to herself. She then went on: "Joseph and Nicodemus promised to prepare the body according to our laws before the Passover feast begins, and I'm certain they are performing that act of supreme love even as we speak." She continued: "There is a huge stone that will be rolled into a deep rut in front of the tomb which will seal it forever. Because they fear a riot or some other type of uprising, and to prevent anyone from robbing the tomb, the High Priest has dispatched guards to guard the tomb. The men were hand-picked by the captain of the guard, the High Priest's most trusted men. And it's a good thing, too, because it will take at least ten big strong men to roll that huge stone down into the rut. Once that stone is in place, though, it will take at least a hundred legionnaires to move it. Because of its weight and the softness of the mossy ground in the garden, that stone will settle into the earth, where it will likely remain forever. And just to be certain there is no trickery of any sort, once the stone is in place, Caiaphas' men will place his own seal between the tomb and the stone, so that if anyone tries to move it, the seal will be broken."

Clearly weary and about to collapse, Mary quietly turned to Peter and said to the group: "Before we partake of the food and drink that this woman has so kindly brought to us, perhaps Simon Peter, our Rock, will lead us in prayer." This was not only a show of respect for Peter, but it was also a signal that from here on out Peter was, without question, the head Disciple, the leader of Christ's Disciples. Peter at first looked at a loss for words. He clearly understood the importance of what the mother of Jesus had done. She had anointed him the leader of all the Disciples, and he fully understood the gravity of this position. As he let this sink in, his gaze went around the room, looking each and every person square in the face, peering into their souls.

He motioned to Toby to go to the table and bring him one of the loaves of bread. Toby brought him the bread and stood right next to him, ready to serve. Peter took the bread, then held it above his head, said a silent prayer, and then said, "Father we thank Thee for this bread which we have received from Your bounty, and we ask Your blessings upon the hands that made it." He then slowly, deliberately broke off a piece of the loaf and said, "When our Lord had taken the bread and given thanks, he broke it and gave it to us, saying, 'Take and eat. This is my body which was given for you. Do this in remembrance of me.'" As Peter spoke these words he moved around the room giving each person a piece of the bread and repeating the statement to each one. Even Toby!

Then he took the jug of wine and did the same thing, saying a silent prayer and giving thanks. Then he again went from person to person, giving each some wine, saying, "Then he took a cup, and when he had given thanks he gave it to us, saying, 'Drink from it, all of you. This is my blood, the blood of the New Covenant, which is poured out for you and for many, for the forgiveness of sins. Do this in remembrance of me.'"

The feeling in the room seemed to have changed. It had been sad, pained, and burdened with grief, each individual person suffering in his or her own way. But now it seemed a little different. Now there was kinship among them, a sense of togetherness. There was now a little glimmer of hope as they shared in this holy communion together. They were brought together as one by sharing in the partaking of wine and bread. This reminded Toby of when Jesus said that whenever two or more gather in his name, he is there. He even imagined his friend being there with them, and the thought comforted him.

His reverie was broken, however, when he looked up and saw Mary, the mother of Jesus, looking right at him, smiling. Ordinarily he'd be frightened at such a thing, but as he looked at her face he felt a warmth spreading through him, an immediate connection to this woman he had never met before. She slowly walked over to him and knelt right in front of him. Ordinarily, this would have frightened him too, but he somehow felt comfortable and at peace. She smiled at him and quietly whispered, "And he is with you, lo, until the end of time, Toby." It was like she had read his mind!

She quickly stood and said, "We have the honor of having one of Jesus' helpers here among us. Jesus loved children, and he loved this young boy," she said. "He often quoted from the Psalmist: 'Out of the mouth of babes and infants hast Thou ordained strength because of Thine enemies, that Thou might still the enemy and the avenger.' He loved to say that those whose innocence is like a child will see the Kingdom of Heaven. For those of you who have yet to meet him, this is Master Toby, and I believe he has something to say."

Toby didn't even think about how scared he ought to be. He was oddly at ease, and he felt such a strong bond of kinship with the people gathered there that he just stepped forward with all the confidence in the world and said, "The last time I was with Jesus I was overcome with sadness and a terrible sense of loss as he told me what was going to happen to him. He told me there would be a time for sorrow, but there would also soon be a time for joy and to try to focus on the joy and not dwell on the sorrow." He looked around the room and felt that feeling again, that feeling of God's love washing over him. He looked at each face, just as he had seen Peter do, and then slowly, deliberately said: "He said to me that whenever two or more gather in his name, he is there with us. And then he said, 'I am with you always, lo, until the end of time.'"

    A calm seemed to settle over the room, and after a few moments Peter said, "And since we are gathered in his name, let us all pray the prayer he taught us," and in unison they said:

Our Father in Heaven,
Hallowed be Your name.
Your Kingdom come,
Your will be done,
on earth as it is in Heaven.
Give us today our daily bread,
and forgive us our debts
as we also have forgiven our debtors.
And lead us not into temptation,
but deliver us from the evil one.

Amen

The Love of a Friend

"Joseph of Arimathea, a prominent member of the Council, who was himself waiting for the kingdom of God, went boldly
to Pilate and asked for Jesus' body."

Mark 15:43

J OHN MARK WAS BETTER. WHEN he awoke this morning he was
bright and alert, and his spirits were good. And Toby was right
there when he awakened. John Mark looked at him and simply
said, "Hi Toby, how are you?"

"How am I?" said Toby. "How am I? Well, I'm great, now
that you're better! I've been worried sick about you!" he exclaimed.
He was dying to talk to John Mark and tell him all the things he'd
missed, but he knew from personal experience that there were certain
types of news that were best heard from your mom, so he went to
get the Widow Mary. He jumped up, whooped with glee, shouted
"Welcome back!", slapped John Mark on the back, and flew across
the room and down the stairs shouting, "He's awake! He's awake!
Miss Mary, he's awake!"

He rounded the corner into the cooking area and almost ran
right smack into Mary. She smiled and heaved a great sigh, and said,
"Well at least those prayers were answered." She slowed Toby down
and asked him to take a moment to pray with her. Toby quieted
down immediately and bowed his head in silence. She said, "Dear
Lord, we thank you for delivering John Mark from his illness, and

for sending him back to us whole and well. Please watch over us in our trials and give us the strength to meet the challenges facing us. We ask this, Father, in the name of your son and our Lord, Jesus."

"Wow!" exclaimed Toby, "that was beautiful, Miss Mary."

"Thank you," said Mary. She could tell that Toby could barely contain himself, so she said, "Just give me a few minutes, Toby. I know you're dying to talk with John Mark, but so am I. And there are some things I have to tell him that will take a little time for him to digest. I'm sure he is eager to see you and talk to you as well, but you'll just have to wait. Peter and John and Mary have gone down to Bethany to meet with the others, but they'll be back this evening when the Sabbath ends. It would be helpful, though, if you would go up to the Temple and tell his rabbi that he is well and will be resuming his studies in a couple of days. But be aware that the Temple will be packed because of the High Holiday. If anyone stops you or gives you any trouble, just show them your mezuzah and you'll be fine."

"I'm already on my way," cried Toby. Then, thinking back to when his mom had told him about his dad, he added, "but actually I think it's going to take more than a few minutes. I'll have plenty of time to spend with John Mark. It's important for him to have this time with you. I'll find his rabbi and use the time to pester him with some questions I've been saving up."

"Why thank you, Toby," she said, "that is very thoughtful of you. John Mark certainly found himself a good friend when he found you."

"I think I'm on the winning end of this friendship," said Toby, "and we have Jesus to thank for that!" He suddenly stopped. Mary looked down at him and saw his eyes were filled with tears. Recognizing he was so very far away from his own mother, Mary got down on her knees and pulled him up against her and just enveloped him in a long, loving, reassuring hug. "This is just something we're all going to have to get used to," she said. "I know it's painful, but we have to stay together and support each other, and remember what he said."

"Whenever two or more of us gather in his name, he is with us," said Toby. "Lo, until the end of time," Mary added. Toby looked up at Mary's face and touched her on the cheek and said, almost in a whisper, "That means he's right here with us right now, Miss Mary, so you can go. You go tend to your son. Jesus and I will be fine right here." At this, it was the Widow Mary whose eyes filled with tears. Finding no words to express her feelings at that moment, she simply hugged the little boy once more, turned, and made her way up the stairs.

As Toby had suspected, the "few minutes" turned into several hours. He stayed around the Temple, just taking in the sights, smells, and sounds, and returned to the house right around lunchtime. He sat at the foot of the stairs, and before too long Mary came down. "Toby," she exclaimed, "I just took John Mark a tray of food for his lunch, fresh bread, delicious figs and olives, and a beautiful red pomegranate. If you hurry, you can probably get there before it's all gone."

"How is he?" asked Toby.

"Physically, he's fine," she said. "Emotionally, though, it will likely take him a while to fully digest the things that have happened. The best thing you can do for him is to keep things light and just be yourself, be the friend that he loves. Have fun."

"That I can do," said Toby. "That just comes naturally to me. In fact, that's what I'm best at!" And with that, he bounded up the stairs calling out to his friend.

Toby and John Mark took the tray of food and sat under the large cluster of pomegranate trees for the rest of the afternoon talking about the events of the past few days. It was the Sabbath, so no one was traveling on the road and there was very little activity in the city. It was rarely this quiet and peaceful, and Toby noticed it had a calming effect on him.

"Where is he now?" asked John Mark.

"Well," said Toby, "I wasn't there, but they told me Joseph of Arimathea went to Pontius Pilate and asked to take possession of Jesus' body. He explained that there were certain rituals that had to be performed, and with the Sabbath approaching there wasn't much time."

"That's true," said John Mark. "Since the time of Abraham, burial has been one of the most sacred of our customs. And the rituals involved can indeed take a lot of time, so I'm sure they were under some pressure to complete them before sundown, when the Passover Sabbath began," John Mark explained. "So what did Pilate say?" he asked.

"Pilate agreed!" said Toby.

"Wow!" exclaimed John Mark. "Either Joseph has amazing powers of persuasion or Pilate is getting soft in his old age. Or, as wealthy as Joseph is, perhaps he bribed Pilate. Most likely, though, Pilate just wanted to get it over with because he was afraid there might be trouble if he said no."

"Probably so," said Toby. "But first Pilate sent the Roman centurion, Cornelius is his name I believe, over to Golgotha to make sure that Jesus was actually dead. He wanted to make sure that this wasn't a trick to sneak Jesus away and tend to him until he got better and then parade him around, claiming he'd been resurrected. Cornelius reported back to Pilate that Jesus really was dead, and then helped Joseph of Arimathea and Nicodemus carry Jesus' body back to Joseph's home."

John Mark turned abruptly and simply stared out into space. Toby didn't know what to think, so he kept quiet for a few moments, but he could only take the silence for so long, so he quietly asked John Mark if something was wrong. John Mark slowly turned to face Toby, tears streaming from his eyes. "To make sure he was really dead . . . to make sure he was really dead . . . Toby," he cried. "I just can't believe Jesus is dead . . . I just can't believe it."

"I'm so sorry, John Mark," said Toby, tears beginning to well up in his own eyes. "I keep forgetting you just learned of all this a few hours ago. It must be completely overwhelming for you."

Within a few moments, the Widow Mary arrived to take John Mark back to the house to check him out and to have him take his medicine. When she saw the grief on John Mark's face, and looked at Toby, she was unable to contain her own grief, and she broke down as well. Toby soon found himself in a group hug with John Mark and the Widow Mary as the three of them grieved together. After a few minutes the Widow Mary squeezed the boys tight, stood up and steeled herself, and said, "Boys, I think we're all overwhelmed and don't know exactly how to come to grips with the events of the past few days, but we will. We will because that's what he would want from us." She turned to Toby and said, "I'm sure there's a lot more you need to tell John Mark, so you just wait right here and I'll bring him back just as soon as he's had his medicine." Toby silently nodded, and as they walked back to the house his thoughts turned once again to Jesus and the profound sadness he felt at the loss of his friend.

CHAPTER 22

Burying a Friend

"Taking Jesus' body, the two of them wrapped
it, with the spices, in strips of linen...there
was a garden and in the garden a new tomb,
in which no one had ever been laid."

John 19:40-41

JOHN MARK SEEMED TO BE a little more energized when he returned to the shade of the pomegranate trees and joined Toby, but Toby knew it wouldn't last. After all, it was just yesterday that the boy was still delirious with fever. But for the moment John Mark was energized and inquisitive. "So tell me," he cried excitedly, "what happened? Finish the story."

"Well," said Toby, "Cornelius, the Roman centurion, helped Joseph and Nicodemus take the body to Joseph's garden. Apparently there's a tomb carved into a little hillside there that Joseph had intended for himself, but he wanted Jesus buried there."

"I know that place!" exclaimed John Mark. "I've been there before, when I was exploring. Actually, don't tell anyone, but I've been there a few times. I know it well."

Toby eyed John Mark with surprise and said, "Tell me about it."

"It's just down the road a bit from Golgotha," said John Mark, "and just a little ways off the road. It's surrounded by dense woods, full of thick cypress trees and scrub. You turn onto this little trail that goes off the road, then cross through the woods, and there's this little clearing that butts up against a little hillside, and that's it. It's a beautiful garden," continued John Mark, "with lots of flowers and flowering bushes. It smells wonderful in the spring when everything is in bloom. There's a very large limestone outcropping coming out of the hillside at the back, and that's where Joseph carved out the tomb. And just outside the entrance to the tomb is the biggest boulder I've ever seen! That's what they'll use to seal up the tomb after he's buried in there. I haven't seen a whole lot of tombs, but Joseph's is pretty big, and there's an opening about chest high and a bit more than shoulder wide, and you kind of step down into it, and…"

"Wait a minute!" cried Toby. "You actually went in there?"

"Yes," said John Mark. "It's okay. It wasn't unclean according to our law, because no one had ever been buried in it."

"Clean, unclean, that's not the point!" cried Toby. "I was thinking about actually going down into a tomb. Even if there was no one in it, it seems kind of spooky."

"A little," said John Mark. "I'm not even sure why I went in there. There was really no reason to, but I felt like it was something I maybe ought to do. And it was daytime, so it wasn't too bad. It would be a lot spookier in the dark. But even in the daytime it's dark in there. There's a ledge that runs along the left wall all the way to the back. I guess that's where you would lay the body. And then on the other side there's a much shorter little ledge that goes about halfway back. I don't know if Joseph is married, but I always just assumed that the shorter one might be for his wife."

He looked up and Toby was just staring at him. "Enough about this stuff," he said impatiently, "now finish your story."

"Okay, okay," said Toby. "John the Disciple brought Jesus' mother back here to your house, but the other women followed Joseph and Nicodemus so they would know exactly where the tomb was. They stood at a distance and watched the men wrap Jesus' body in a long linen sheet, placing layers of spices and perfumes between the folds of linen. With sundown approaching quickly, the men had to hurry. They tried to pick up the body, but wrapped into the linen with all the spices, it was too heavy for them. They sent for Nicodemus' son to come and help them, and with his help they laid the body up on the ledge and placed a small square piece of linen over the facial area. Salome says they were such a distance away that they couldn't tell if the preparations were complete, because they were done in such haste. She isn't sure they were done in full accordance with the Law, so she and Mary of Magdala plan to go back there first thing in the morning after the Sabbath to finish up. But they're going to have a difficult time of it, I'm afraid."

"Why is that?" asked John Mark.

"Because," said Toby, "just as the men laid the body up on the ledge, a group of Temple guards showed up, men hand-picked by Caiaphas. Their leader was the captain of the guard, the High Priest's most trusted man. This was just the four-man advance team from the Temple, several more would follow. Pilate had also arranged for a contingent of fifteen of his own Roman soldiers to stand guard. They had a written document signed by Pilate instructing them to stand guard over the tomb for the next two days, and it also commanded Joseph to allow them to stay there and to let them build warming fires during the hours of darkness. The guards were instructed to roll the stone into place and to put a seal bearing the mark of Pilate between the rock and the front of the tomb so they would know if anyone tried to raid it."

"But why would anyone do that?" queried John Mark. "Tombs that contain the dead are terribly unclean! They're so unclean that even to stand in the shadow of a tomb will make you unclean and you'll to have to undergo all manner of purification rituals in order to be cleansed. And with Passover so close, you wouldn't be able to enter the Temple, because there isn't time to get purified. No self-respecting Jew would get near an occupied tomb, much less enter it!"

"Well," replied Toby, "I heard Mary of Magdala say that Caiaphas and the authorities are afraid that Jesus' followers, especially the Disciples, will come and steal the body and say he's been resurrected."

"Hah! The Disciples," jeered John Mark. "I heard they're down in Bethany, for goodness' sake. They're afraid to show their faces in Jerusalem, much less pull off some daring grave robbery!" he said, laughing.

"Well, apparently Caiaphas believes them to be more courageous than they are," said Toby, "because he's afraid they will take the body and hide it to make it seem like Jesus' prophesies of rising from the grave have actually been fulfilled. That would cause more and more people to believe in Jesus, and might even cause the people to riot, both of which would be bad for him. So he has posted the Temple guards and sealed the tomb to make sure nothing like that happens. I think he's safe, though, because nobody's going to get into that tomb."

"Why is that?" asked John Mark.

"Well, you've been there, you've seen the stone," said Toby, "so you know how large it is! Joseph and the others had a good laugh at the Temple guards' expense when four of them tried to roll the stone down into the rut to seal the tomb, and they weren't even able to budge it one inch! They couldn't do a thing with it until the other guards and fifteen Roman soldiers showed up. And when they were finally able to move the stone, it settled down into the rut almost a foot, it's so heavy." He added, "That's why I said that Mary and Salome are likely to have a hard time of it in the morning. Even if they take all eleven Disciples with them they'll still have to get the guards to help them, if they even will. They were going to go to the Temple to get Caiaphas' permission for his men to help as well, but it was beginning to turn dark and they had to hurry home for the Sabbath."

Evening was approaching. Toby looked over at John Mark and saw his friend was sagging down in his chair, obviously weary and tiring quickly. "Oh my gosh!" he exclaimed. "John Mark, I am so sorry, I've just been going on and on in my excitement without a thought about how tired you must be. I'm afraid I've worn you out with my yapping," he said. "Instead of listening to me go on and on you should be resting. Let's get you back to the house and in bed."

John Mark didn't respond right away. Instead, once again he seemed to stare off into space, in another world. Just as Toby was about to ask if he was all right, John Mark turned his head to face him. Toby was a little alarmed at John Mark's expression. "You look like you've just seen a ghost," he said.

John Mark said, "You are right, Toby, I'm tired, very tired. But it's not just that. So much has happened—so many things have happened while I was sick, and I guess I'm also still a bit overwhelmed by it all."

"I can see why you would be," said Toby. "I'm sorry I added to it by telling you all these things. Your mother told me to take things slow and easy, but in my excitement over you being well, I guess I just got carried away. Forgive me, please," he added.

"Oh, it's not that," said John Mark. "And if it were, I would certainly forgive you. I would even forgive you seventy times seven if need be," he added with a wink.

"Aha, so you heard about my conversation with Mary Magdalene?" said Toby.

"Of course I heard. I'm the writer of stories; you can't hide anything from me." John Mark laughed as he said this but then quickly went into a wrenching coughing spasm, barely able to catch his breath.

"That's it!" cried Toby. "We're going to get you back into the house and in bed right now!"

The coughing subsided, and John Mark quietly said, "Wait, Toby, wait just a second." He caught his breath and looked at Toby. In his face Toby saw weariness, to be sure, but also worry and deep concern.

"What is it?" Toby asked.

"It's just a feeling I have, Toby," he said. "I can't explain it, but something tells me it's not over yet. Just a feeling, but I've learned to trust my feelings. I just sense that something is going to happen."

"You're just exhausted," said Toby reassuringly. "Once you rest up and get some food in you for a change, I'm sure you'll feel better."

"That may be," said John Mark, "but if something does happen and you and I get separated, or if something should happen and you're scared, be sure to keep your mezuzah close to your heart. Hold onto it and just pray, and things will work out; it will be okay."

Toby nodded. John Mark fell silent for a few moments, thinking, and then said, "You said the guards had permission to build warming fires, didn't you?"

"Yes," said Toby. "Why?"

"If they light warming fires in the garden," John Mark said, "you'll be able to see them from the terrace. If you draw a straight line from the city gate up the road to Golgotha, you'll see the fires just this side of that awful place. And with the sacrificial fires burning in the Temple for Passover, you'll have a good view of the Temple as well. For some reason I have a feeling you might want to keep an eye on both places this night."

Toby began to experience a sinking feeling in his stomach, too, a feeling that he had been hiding from for over two days. But after John Mark had brought it out into the open he could no longer pretend it wasn't there. In his heart he knew John Mark was right. That indeed it wasn't over yet. Things remained very unsettled, and he felt a vague sense of dread, but he didn't know why. Like there was something out there, something moving toward him, picking up speed as it came. He could sense it getting closer and closer. But he didn't know what it was. He had been sensing it over the past two days. And he knew there was no stopping it, whatever it was. But Toby refused to give in to the fear. Instead, he brushed it aside, put on his happy face and said, "Don't be silly, my friend! You and I have been inseparable since the day we met, and I don't see that changing! At all! And as for the mezuzah, I believe I've already told you, it's the most precious gift anyone has ever given me. I haven't taken it off since you gave it to me. I hold onto it each night when I pray, and you were right—it not only keeps me close to the Father, but it also makes me feel a connection to my father." He then added, "And to your father as well. I promise you that I will keep it near my heart. Always." And then he heard himself say, "Lo, until the end of time."

John Mark looked at him quizzically. Toby shrugged and said, "Just something I heard somewhere, I don't know. You know how it is," as he wondered what in the world had possessed him to say such a thing. Then he jumped up and said, "I'd race you back to the house, but that would be entirely too easy, so give me your arm and let me walk you back there."

John Mark smiled. "After I rest up a bit I'll race you back to the house any time, my friend. You'll be sorry you let this opportunity to beat me slip away, because it will be your last!"

And as a gentle breeze rustled the leaves on the trees and the smell of ripe fruit sweetened the air, the two friends made their way back to the house, laughing all the way.

For the very last time.

SECTION V

Hope Returns

CHAPTER 23

From the Mouths of Babes

"At that time Jesus said, 'I praise you, Father,
Lord of heaven and earth, because you have
hidden these things from the wise and learned,
and revealed them to little children.'"

Matthew 11:25

I T WAS JUST AFTER SUNDOWN, and John Mark was sleeping comfortably. Peter and John had stayed down in Bethany with the others, and Mary, mother of Jesus, had gone to be with her sons, James and Jude. The other Marys and Salome were all downstairs sleeping and would rise early in the morning to go to the tomb to finish the work Joseph and Nicodemus had begun. The Widow Mary was sleeping comfortably for the first time in days now that John Mark was out of danger. The drama, which had been constant since Jesus' triumphal entry into the city, had finally subsided.

And Jesus was dead.

The Son of Man, the Son of the Living God, the Messiah, had been crucified between two common criminals. The descendant of King David, the Chosen One, the Deliverer! The man who was expected to end Roman occupation and oppression and restore Israel to her proper status among nations as the "Handmaiden of God," was dead. Betrayed, abandoned, rejected, scourged, mocked, beaten, and crucified. The shock, horror, fear, and ultimately bottomless sorrow of his followers had run its course, leaving them numb and empty. Just as the Jews had been lost in the wilderness a thousand years before, like sheep wandering aimlessly without a shepherd, Jesus' followers, too, were lost. Many had even talked about returning to their home towns and taking up their former jobs once again. They were dejected and wondered if following Jesus had simply been folly, a waste of time and energy. To see the Son of Man, David's direct descendant, treated like an animal was the last thing they had expected, and they were unsure of how this could be reconciled with Jesus' promises about the Kingdom of Heaven.

Toby finally had a chance to rest. A chance to really rest. He couldn't remember when the house had been so quiet, although it had only been three days. He was in his favorite spot, on the terrace. It was just after sundown and Passover had ended, but there were still many people moving about in the city. Lamps in the windows of the homes along the streets of Jerusalem continued to burn, as did the fires at the Temple, giving the night sky an eerie glow.

Tomorrow morning Jerusalem would be a beehive of activity as all the pilgrims would begin making their way home now that the High Holiday had come to a close. The road below would be alive with the sounds of travelers chatting, people singing, and children playing. Donkeys, camels, dogs, sheep, and many other animals would compete with people for space on the road. Although the High Holiday had passed, the people traveling below would still be joyous, and the air would be filled with singing, chanting, and other happy sounds. Toby wondered if any of them would give a second thought to the lowly carpenter from Nazareth who had been murdered by the very people whose souls he had come here to save.

Toby thought it strange that all the adults, the Disciples, the women, the neighbors, all were despondent and dejected. There was a lot of hand-wringing, crying, and worrying about what the future would bring. Some were afraid. Some were angry. And some just seemed paralyzed. But they all had one thing in common—they seemed to have lost all hope. And yet he and John Mark had not. They both knew without question that Jesus would rise and be resurrected, just as he said he would. After supper they went out and sat on the terrace, talking. They discussed the treachery of Judas, the hypocrisy of the Jewish authorities, and the brutality of the Romans, to be sure. And they spoke wistfully and with great sorrow of the fact that Jesus had been taken from them. But they didn't dwell on these things.

As far as each boy was concerned those were things of the past. Done. Mostly what they talked about was what was to come. They talked about all the times Jesus had prophesied not just his crucifixion, but his resurrection. By the end, Jesus had left no doubt he was indeed the Messiah, the Son of the Living God, and he made it clear that no matter what happened, God was in control. Toby and John Mark had not one iota of doubt that Jesus would be resurrected; and that he would go to prepare a place for them as well. Toby didn't understand why the grown-ups didn't seem to get it. Jesus certainly had said it enough times and in enough different ways.

John Mark said, "They would probably wonder why we feel this way. Why we're not in terrible despair. And why, instead of moping about, we're eagerly awaiting the resurrection." He paused, thoughtfully, then said, in a very small voice, "Sometimes I wonder why myself."

"*Why?*" cried Toby, "*Why?*" He jumped up and threw his head back and shouted, "Because he said so, that's why! He said so! He said not to dwell on the sorrowful, but to look forward, toward the joyous! Because he said that evil would have its day, but that good will win in the end! Because he said that the Father will show everyone, the whole world, that love is greater than hate, that good triumphs over evil! And because he said that even though he dies, he will rise again! Because he said so, John Mark, that's why! Because he said so!" He finally sat down.

John Mark seemed a little taken aback by the intensity of Toby's emotions. To be perfectly honest, Toby was a bit surprised himself. He gathered himself and quietly, but very deliberately, said, "Because he said so, John Mark. Because he said so. What more do we need than that?"

John Mark nodded. Together they came to the conclusion that for some reason it must be easier for children to have faith. They didn't know why, but it just seemed easier for them to believe than it did for grown-ups. But dusk was soon upon them and Toby could see that John Mark was getting fatigued, so on that note the two made their way back inside. John Mark went right to sleep. Toby went back out to his place on the terrace, but he didn't sleep.

In the quiet of the terrace Toby was reflecting on their conversation, and especially about why it seemed that the two young boys found it easier to believe than did many of the adults. And then it came to him: *So that's what he meant when he said "the Kingdom of God belongs to such as these."* This triggered other memories. Just this morning Mary, mother of Jesus, had said how much he loved the psalm that said, "From the lips of children and infants, you, Lord, have called forth your praise." And then he remembered the time that Matthew, the former tax collector, told him about Jesus denouncing the towns where he had performed great works, because they did not repent and change their ways. Matthew said that Jesus said, "I praise you, Father, Lord of heaven and earth, because You have hidden these things from the wise and learned, and revealed them to little children."

I suppose that's why he needs people like me and John Mark to be his helpers, thought Toby. While he found some satisfaction and comfort in this thought, he still wondered what it meant to be a helper. Jesus often reassured him that his help would be important, but Toby just didn't see it. Then he remembered Jesus saying that he could be helping in many ways and not even be aware of it, which he supposed might be true. He knew he shouldn't, but he just couldn't help wishing that he could have played a more important role in things, and that he could have been of more value to Jesus. After a great deal of thought he came to the conclusion that it really didn't matter. It didn't matter what he wanted or what might make him feel bigger or more valued. He knew that however God chose to use him, he would take on the task with joy in his heart, no matter how small or meaningless the task might seem to him at the time.

Just then he saw the light of a new fire being lit. This one was way up the road on the other side of the city, out near Golgotha. Toby reckoned it was in Joseph's garden, where the body of Jesus lay. The guards sent by the authorities to guard the tomb must have started the fire to warm themselves, he supposed. Then he noticed four much smaller fires moving in different directions, and decided that the four guards on watch must have lit torches so they would be able to see anyone approaching the garden. As he watched the torches moving in the night his thoughts turned to Jesus and the time they had spent together. These memories were fresh in his mind, because he had been reporting them to John Mark to include in his stories. He recalled their first meeting by the River Jordan and how the clouds parted when John baptized Jesus and the dove landed on his shoulder. He thought about the time they spent in the wilderness, and how Jesus stood up to Satan and didn't give an inch. And though he tried not to, he thought about the fiercely ugly, but incredibly gentle angel that attended Jesus after Satan left in defeat. He thought about walking on the water in the Sea of Galilee, how Jesus calmed the storm, and the feeding of the five thousand. And mostly he thought about the talks he had with Jesus atop the thinking rock and other places they had traveled.

Lost in his reverie, Toby didn't notice the city becoming darker. Gradually the lights in the windows of homes along the city streets were extinguished as people went to sleep and prepared for a new day tomorrow. The fires in the Temple were slowly dying, casting a low glow inside the Temple interrupted only by occasional sparks lifted up on the wind. As he became more fully aware of his surroundings, Toby noticed that the only fires still burning brightly were the torches and the warming fire of the men guarding Jesus' tomb. Though it was still fairly early in the evening, Toby's eyelids grew heavy. He wanted to stay awake just in case anything should happen, so he could be there if he was needed. He tried valiantly to stay awake, but it was a losing battle. Soon he dropped off into a restless, fitful sleep.

CHAPTER 24

A Strange Visitor

"They will kill him, and on the third
day he will be raised to life."
Matthew 17:23

T OBY WAS AWAKENED BY LOUD noises coming from down the
hill. He tried to get up, but his sleep had been so fitful that he
had wrapped himself up in his blankets, like he was in a cocoon.
The moon was still mostly full, and he reckoned by the position of
the moon that it was about midnight. When he looked down he was
amazed at how he had managed to tangle himself up in his covers.
By the time he finally unraveled himself he could hear the noises
much more clearly—they were voices. Just one voice, actually, but it
was loud, coarse, and quite angry. He ran over to the corner of the
courtyard overlooking the palace of Caiaphas, the High Priest, but he
couldn't see down there because the steep hillside was in the way. He
scrambled up a cypress tree until he was high up enough to see below.

It was Caiaphas and several of his bodyguards, coming toward
the palace from the Temple. They were probably returning after
Caiaphas finished his duties as High Priest. It was hard to tell what
he was angry about, but he was really letting two of the Temple
guards have it, calling them all sorts of names and threatening them
with most unpleasant consequences if they didn't straighten up and
straighten up fast. "You were there!" he shouted. "You were there!" he
shouted again. Toby figured the second shout was for dramatic effect.
"How could you have let that happen? How could you have let the

Arimathean take custody of the body. Why didn't anyone come and tell me?"

"We couldn't," said the guard. "You were engaged in prayer and the ritual preparations for the sacrifice and could not be disturbed! We tried, but were turned away by your attendants. We even went to the home of Annas to try to get him to intervene, but his orderlies turned us away as well," the soldier cried.

"Well, you should have done something, even if you had to do it on your own authority. If you had just done something," Caiaphas continued, "this never would have happened. That miserable Jesus would have been tossed into a roadside grave along with those two miserable criminals he was crucified alongside of. Pilate, that snake!" Caiaphas ranted. "He would do anything to get under my skin! He knew I would never allow the Arimathean or any other Jew to claim Jesus' body. He said over and over again that he would be resurrected from the dead. That isolated garden is the perfect spot for a grave robbery! They could sneak in there and steal his body and then claim to all that he had been raised!"

He stopped to take a breath, but it was not a calming breath: "That little snake!" he cried. "If the body had been thrown in the ditch with those other two criminals no one would ever expect him to be resurrected. Son of God indeed! If they had seen their Son of God lying in a ditch sandwiched between two criminals they'd give up that notion of a resurrection lickety-split, that's for sure! But no!" he continued. "Pilate agrees to the Arimathean's outlandish request. I know he dispatched a group of his soldiers to guard the tomb, but I don't trust them either. So I had to post a group of my own best men, just to make sure those ragamuffin Disciples of his don't rob it and hide the body away." He then softened a bit, saying, almost to himself, "But that's all right . . . the Nazarene will lay in that tomb, and he won't get out. I'll see to that. And after six or seven weeks everything will be back to normal. Everyone will forget they even heard the name Jesus of Nazareth."

Then, catching himself softening, he quickly turned toward his guards and spat, "Out! Out of my sight! Why don't you go work for Pilate, you traitorous snakes! Out of my sight!" And he stormed up the steps of the palace and disappeared.

The guards walked directly toward Toby and turned down the road right under his perch in the tree. "Whew!" he heard one of them say. "I was afraid he'd have our heads for this. If a good dressing down is all that comes out of this, we should consider ourselves quite fortunate indeed."

"Agreed," said one of the others, adding, "I guess this time Pilate got him good," trying to suppress a little chuckle. The others soon joined in the laughter, relieved to be leaving with their heads still attached to their bodies. They passed out of sight, and while Toby could no longer see them, he could still hear their chuckling through the quiet night air.

Toby climbed down from his perch and made his way back to the terrace, suddenly finding his eyelids drooping once again. He had barely gotten onto the terrace before falling into a deep, deep sleep. Sometime later he was awakened by a low moan. He looked up, and saw that a thick fog had settled over the city. Just when he thought it must have been a dream, he heard it again. The moaning seemed to come closer and closer, and then a figure slowly appeared through the mist. A person! As the figure drew closer, Toby saw it was a man, dressed only in a loincloth.

Toby was frightened. In the most courageous voice he could muster he said, "W-W-Who are you? And w-w-w-what are you doing here?" Silence. Toby asked again, this time a little more courageously, "Who are you? Are you okay? What are you doing here?" Then, after a pause he asked, "Is there something I can do for you?"

Toby heard a voice saying, "Tell them where to meet me," but he didn't see the man's mouth move or anything, and he didn't recognize the voice.

Bewildered, he said, "What? What do you want me to do?"

The figure slowly turned and disappeared through the mist, and all Toby heard was, "Tell them where to meet me," again.

Toby stood to see if he could see the man. When he looked down he saw a linen cloth, like a linen napkin or something that the man had dropped onto the terrace floor. Toby picked it up and started to run after the man, calling out, "Sir, you dropped this!" when he suddenly realized he was about to run right off the terrace. He stopped abruptly and just stared through the mist. He absent-mindedly tucked the napkin into his loincloth under his nightshirt. He sat back down on his bedclothes and closed his eyes, and then it hit him—that man walked right off the terrace and into space! He walked right off the terrace!

Toby sat bolt upright and opened his eyes. The mist was gone. The sky was clear and illuminated by the light of the near-full moon. There were billions of stars in the sky, and a gentle breeze wafted through the leaves of the trees around him. *Whew!* he thought. *It really was just a dream, just a dream!* By the position of the moon Toby reckoned it to be about three o'clock in the morning. He still felt a bit disoriented from the dream, so he stood up to take some deep breaths and decided to climb down and walk around the court-yard a bit to clear his head. He looked up the road to the north and again saw the light from the warming fire in Joseph's garden, but he didn't see any torches. *That's odd,* he thought, *maybe they're just back in the cypress woods and I can't see them.*

He moved off the terrace and over to the edge of the courtyard overlooking Caiaphas' palace to get a better look. Just then he saw a light flicker just inside the northern gate into the city. And then another! And they were moving fast, as though the people carrying them were running. They disappeared into the darkness for a while, but then emerged again and were getting closer, heading down the street to the palace of Caiaphas, coming right at Toby. They were chattering excitedly, but they were too far away for Toby to hear what they were saying. For the second time tonight he climbed up to his perch in the tree and quietly waited.

CHAPTER 25

He Is Risen!

"But when they looked up, they
saw that the stone, which was very
large, had been rolled away.
As they entered the tomb, they saw a young
man dressed in a white robe sitting on
the right side, and they were alarmed."

Mark 16:5

TOBY DIDN'T HAVE TO WAIT long, for the men were running at full speed. As they neared the palace of Caiaphas, two of the men carrying the torches slowed, but the other two kept on going heading for the gate and out of the city. "Hey," cried one on the palace guards, "where do you think you're going?"

"Out of this city, never to return," came the reply. "Never!" shouted the other.

The one from the steps cried, "He wasn't resurrected, don't be silly . . . we just fell asleep and they came and stole his body, and now they're probably hiding it somewhere."

"Fine," came a voice out of the darkness, "you tell Caiaphas that! Resurrected or not, that tomb is empty, and we're not going to spend the rest of our lives in prison."

But the other man began chanting, "He is resurrected! He is risen! Our Lord has been resurrected, just as he promised," and that voice echoed off the hillsides as the men ran down the road toward Bethany.

Toby could hardly believe his ears! First the dream, and now this? He pinched himself to make sure he wasn't still dreaming. "Ouch!" he cried. This is real! Wearing nothing but his bleached white nightshirt and loincloth, he raced across the courtyard, hit the road running, and didn't stop until he neared the cypress woods surrounding Joseph's garden. Out of breath and panting, he slowly, silently crept through the woods. With every step he wished more and more he had taken the time to get his sandals.

He wasn't sure the garden was empty. He thought maybe some of the guards might have doused their torches and hidden in the woods, so he moved very stealthily, trying not to make a sound. It must have taken him an hour to cross the dark woods. However, as he moved through the woods, crowded with scrub and sturdy, thick-trunked cypress trees, he became more and more confident he was alone. When he reached the edge of the clearing, in the moonlight he could see all the way across to the hillside on the far side of the garden. And he could barely believe his eyes—the stone had been moved! That huge boulder, taller than a man and as thick as two oxen, the one that sank over a foot into the sod when it was rolled to seal the tomb, had been moved!

Toby was tempted to race directly across the garden to the tomb, but at the last minute he thought better of it. He still didn't know where the guards were, so he crept along the edge of the clearing until he got close to the tomb. Well, by now his excitement had turned to fear. Oh how he wished John Mark were here! Or better yet, Peter, the Rock! But no, he was alone. Gradually though, a realization began to form itself in his mind, and he was comforted—Jesus was risen! Toby knew he would find an empty tomb. He just sensed it. He found himself saying a silent prayer, asking the Father to give him the courage to do what he knew he had to do, and to give him the wisdom to know what he should do next.

He stared at the tomb. Believing his prayer had been heard and answered, he slowly began walking toward the tomb, his bleached nightshirt almost glowing in the moonlight, out in the open for all to see. His knees were wobbly and his whole body was shaking, but he kept walking, straight toward the little opening in the rock. He stopped directly in front of the opening, held his breath, and listened. Nothing. He knelt down and peered inside the tomb to see if he could see any movement. Nothing. Only darkness. He pulled his legs in front of him, sat on his bottom, and slowly began moving into the tomb, down one step and then the other. He sat still for the longest time, just listening to the silence and letting his eyes adjust to the darkness.

When he could see a little better he gathered his nerve and stood, directly facing the shelf on which he almost half expected to find the body of Jesus. But it wasn't there! And what was there on the ledge gave Toby a start, for it seemed quite unnatural. On that shelf was a long piece of linen, wrapped numerous times as though wrapped around a body. Leaning over close to the linen, Toby could smell and see traces of the spices that had been placed between the folds of the linen by Joseph and Nicodemus in their preparations. The whole cloth was completely undisturbed! It looked as though there had actually once been a body wrapped up in it, but the body had been removed—not unwrapped, just removed. The only thing missing, aside from the body, was the linen cloth that the women had said the men used to cover Jesus' head—that was nowhere to be found. Toby looked all around the tomb for the cloth, but found nothing. This was perplexing. It just didn't make sense that everything else would be perfect, just as it had been when they laid Jesus there, but no cloth anywhere.

Toby stood back and placed his hands on his hips in frustration. When he did so, he felt an odd bulge at his waist. He lifted his nightshirt up above his loincloth and remembered the thing the man dropped on the terrace in his dream. *Wait a minute!* thought Toby. *That was a dream!* He slowly reached in and pulled out the cloth that had been dropped on the terrace. He looked at it, felt it, and smelled it, and it smelled just like the linen wrap on the shelf! Toby moved closer to the opening of the tomb to examine the cloth more closely in the moonlight. When he looked down on it, he saw an almost-perfect face of Jesus! Right there on the cloth! This was the cloth that had been laid over his face! *But . . . but . . . ,* thought Toby as he began to swoon, his knees buckling and his vision blurring. *But that was just a dream!* This was his last thought before he staggered backward and passed out right there on the floor of the tomb.

After what seemed to him to be hours, Toby slowly regained consciousness. While it was still dark outside, he could tell that the dawn was not too very far away. As he gathered his senses he just stared at the shelf with complete awe. "This is the very spot where they laid the body of my Lord and Savior, Jesus Christ. My friend," he spoke aloud, startled by the sound of his own voice. He began to pray, thanking the Father for delivering His son from his enemies, for lifting Jesus up out of his agony and returning him to Paradise. And for sending His son to atone for our sins and through God's grace granting us everlasting life. He opened his eyes and just sat there on the low shelf for the longest time as though in a trance, feeling the power of the tomb and of the resurrected Jesus, confident that what he had experienced was not really a dream, but a vision—a vision of the risen Christ! He almost fainted again at this revelation!

It was early, just about an hour before dawn, when Salome awakened James' mother and Mary of Magdala, whispering, "Mary, Mary, wake up, we've work to do." The women immediately rose from their cots and knelt in prayer. When they finished, Mary of Magdala went out the back way, by the cooking area, and picked up a basket with perfumes and spices in it. Mary the mother of James picked up the smaller basket right beside it. When they arrived out in the rear courtyard Salome was already there, with a long linen cloth rolled up and resting on her shoulder. They silently made their way out onto the road and began moving through the city before either spoke.

Salome said, "I noticed that Peter and the others made their way back here during the night, I almost tripped over John when I awoke. I'm glad to see they made it back safely."

Mary of Magdala said, "Yes, they didn't mean to, but they woke me when they came in. They were terribly weary and quite sorrowful and downhearted. I washed their feet and brought them blankets to keep warm, and each man immediately set about finding his own sleeping place. No talk, no request for food or drink, just right to sleep," she said.

Mary, mother of James, said, "And I slept through the whole thing! I must have been exhausted." Although the others had tried to discourage them, the women were determined to see that their Lord had been laid to rest according to their Law. This was a labor of love on their part, a show of deep respect. They had no criticism of Nicodemus and Joseph if it turned out they were unable to complete the rituals correctly—there simply wasn't enough time before the Sabbath started.

Dawn was still about a half-hour away when they reached the garden. They were surprised to find there were no guards there. They looked across the moonlit garden, and each saw the sight at the very same moment. Salome gasped and fell to her knees, as did Mary, mother of James. But Mary of Magdala just dropped everything and raced across the garden, running right at the open tomb. "Wait for us!" cried the other two as they recovered and began running to catch up. They reached Mary just as she began to bend over to try and peer into the darkened chamber. Salome placed her hand on the small of Mary's back, with James' mother doing the same to her, both standing on tiptoe, trying to see around Mary and into the tomb.

Just as they peered over Mary's shoulder the women heard this startled yelp from within the tomb, which just about frightened them out of their wits. All three women screamed in fright at the same time. As Mary quickly straightened up, she inadvertently threw poor Salome and James' mother to the ground, still screaming. She helped them up and all three women ran as fast as they could across the garden. They were making so much noise they barely heard the boy calling out to them.

Salome turned when she heard a voice call out. She saw a young boy wearing the whitest robe she had ever seen. She thought he must be an angel. As she turned she heard him say, "Don't be afraid. You seek Jesus of Nazareth who was crucified. He is risen! He is not here. Behold the place where they have laid him. But go, tell his Disciples and Peter, 'He is going ahead of you into Galilee. There will you see him, just as he told you.'"

The women ran all the way through the city to the home of the Widow Mary. They burst into the home and jostled Peter and the others, excitedly telling the men their tale.

"It was an angel, I tell you," said Mary of Magdala, "a young boy, all dressed in white, an angel, sitting on the ledge inside the tomb in a white robe."

The men looked skeptical, but then Salome said, "I saw him too! It was just as Mary described." And then she told them what the young man had said.

Toby was startled out of his reverie by the sounds of voices coming across the garden. He felt the cold stone floor against his back and quickly raised himself onto the lower shelf toward the rear of the tomb. It took him a few moments to fully get his wits about him, and he thought perhaps he should get up and investigate. He looked up and saw a figure filling the little entrance to the tomb, silhouetted against the early dawn. Startled, he cried out, and when he did, so did the person who had peered into the tomb. Toby heard other screams and realized they were women. He got to his feet and made his way to the opening, but by then the women were all the way across the courtyard, running with their backs to him. He called out, "Don't be afraid. You seek Jesus of Nazareth who was crucified. He is risen! He is not here. Behold the place where they have laid him. But go, tell his Disciples and Peter, 'He is going ahead of you into Galilee. There will you see him, just as he told you.'"

He sat back down on the shelf, confused. And then it hit him. That must have been the Marys and Salome, come to complete the ritual burial for their Lord. His very next thought was that the guards would hear them running through the city, screaming and carrying on! He panicked, fearing that either Caiaphas' men or the Romans would come to the garden to investigate and when they found him there they would arrest him . . . or worse!

He bolted up off the shelf and out of the tomb and started running back to the Widow Mary's home just as fast as his little legs would carry him. His head was down and his little legs were churning just as fast as they could, which is why he didn't see the tree—that big, thick-trunked cypress tree right at the edge of the garden. *Wham!* He hit the tree at full speed. He hit the ground hard, landing flat on his back. He felt sick. When he was finally able to open his eyes he actually did see the tree. It was looming above him. He was looking straight up at it. And it was spinning around in circles. In fact, the whole world was spinning around. It made Toby dizzy, so he decided to close his eyes to make it stop. And that's when everything went black.

SECTION VI

Home

CHAPTER 26

Home

"Lo, I am with you always, even unto
the end of the world. Amen."
Matthew 28:20

WHEN TOBY AWOKE HE WAS still lying on his back, looking up. It was daytime, and boy, was it bright. He was looking straight up at a big, bright light. Maybe the brightest daylight he'd ever seen. It hurt his eyes. He was afraid. He closed his eyes, and then it came to him. *People who have those near-death experiences always talk about seeing incredibly bright light, the brightest light ever.* Then it hit him . . . *Oh, no*, he thought, *I'm dead.* Then he looked down. His Sunday School clothes were gone. Instead, he was wearing some kind of robe. His good shoes were gone and on his feet were some kind of booties, like made of paper or something. *Oh, now I get it,* he thought, *I'm not dead! I'm in a hospital. Whew!* Relieved, he laid back down.

Then he heard someone speak his name, but it sounded like it was coming from an echo chamber or something very far away. He thought he heard it again, so he slowly looked up, and when he did he saw people all around him. He heard his name again, but this time he knew who had said it—it was his mom! He sat up quickly, perhaps a little too quickly, as it turned out, and he saw his mom, who was crying. Also there were her sister, two ladies from the neighborhood, and his pastor! Just like when his dad had died. *Oh no*, he thought, *I really am dead, after all.* He felt woozy and felt himself sinking backward again, just like in the tomb. Then he was out.

When he opened his eyes again it was dark outside, but the lights were on in his room. He raised his head and saw the most beautiful face he had ever seen. It had to be an angel! For some reason the image of a fiercely ugly angel popped into his mind, but he quickly dismissed that as a dream he must have had. This face belonged to his mom. And she was smiling and beaming, looking just like she did before. *Before?* thought Toby. *Before what?* But then it dawned on him: *Hey, who cares before what? This is my mom!*

She stood and leaned over him, giving him the biggest hug ever, and said, "Toby, I've been so worried about you. We were all so worried about you."

"How long have I been gone?" asked Toby.

His mom said, "You weren't gone at all, my love, you've been right here for the past three days, but you'll be going home tomorrow."

Toby cried. He hugged his mom around the neck like he would never let her go. He didn't know why, but for some reason he had been afraid he'd never see her again.

He said, "I'm so sorry, Mom, I am so very sorry!"

She sat back and said, "Why Toby, what on earth could you be sorry for?"

Toby held back his tears and said, "For everything. Because I've been so bad. Because of how much pain I've caused you. And because I've been such a rotten kid."

She held him tight, and looked like her heart was breaking.

She said, "Toby, I love you. You've been through a terrible time. No one deserves to go through what you've been through. I know you've been struggling, but you're still the same smart, kind, and lovable boy you've always been, it's just been hard."

She held back tears of her own and said, "I haven't been the kind of mother I'd like to be, either. I've been so busy working and I haven't been able to be with you like I should." After a long pause she quietly said, "I was so worried about you after you got hurt, and to see you lying there like that just broke my heart . . . I would have given anything to have traded places with you so you wouldn't have hurt so badly."

Ding!

Toby thought he heard a bell go off, but he realized it was just in his head. Maybe he had a concussion or something. But for some reason that last statement had struck him deeply, in a most meaningful way, but he didn't know why. He just held on tight, and after a while whispered, "I love you, Mom."

She smiled and said, "And I love you, my Toby. I always have and I always will. I will love you until the end of time."

Ding!!

There it was again. Something again stirred deep inside, something vaguely familiar, but he just couldn't quite put his finger on it. His mom softly said, "Now you get some sleep! I'll be right here in this chair if you need me in the night. And when you wake up tomorrow we'll go home." Before she finished the sentence, Toby was fast asleep.

The next several days were uneventful. Toby's mom took off from work and he got to spend a lot of time with her, just talking, playing games, and watching videos. One evening Toby got ready for bed and his mom came in to say bedtime prayers with him. When they finished Toby said, "I'm sorry I caused you so much worry, Mom. I didn't mean to. I hope you can forgive me for causing you such worry and grief."

She said, "Toby, there's nothing to forgive, but if there were, of course I would forgive you. I always stand ready to forgive you. Like the Bible says, I would forgive you seventy times seven."

Ding!!!

There it was again! That nagging sense of something important within him. He tried to figure out what it was. It was like something familiar, but just barely out of reach. He finally let go of the search when he heard his mom say: "Of course I was worried about you. We all were. You were in a coma and had a serious concussion. But I had faith, Toby. I believed in my heart that you would be all right. I just had faith, and then I wasn't worried any longer."

Toby said, "Faith, huh?"

His mom looked at him with bottomless compassion and said, "Yes, Toby, faith. It's my rock! Faith, hope, and love, that's what our relationship to God is all about."

Ding!!!!

Toby ignored it this time. He had an important question he needed to ask her. He looked up and said: "But how can you have such faith after dad . . . after . . . you know . . .? I mean you could have had all the faith in the world and it still would have happened. How can you have faith after that?"

His mom sat still and silent for what seemed like a very long time. Then she said, "Because that's what faith is, Toby. Faith is believing that God is in control and that we're all part of His plan, and that even if things happen that we can't fathom or we think are terrible, we have to accept that God is still in control. Sometimes He works in strange and mysterious ways to implement His will."

Ding!!!!!

Toby felt like he almost had it, that he could almost grasp the elusive thoughts and memories that kept being triggered. But he just couldn't seem to latch onto them. His mom said, "Now tomorrow is Sunday, and I have the day off, so I'll be going to church with you. We can walk there together and I'll meet you after Sunday School and we can sit together during the church service." Then she added, "I want to tell you, Toby, what a joy it has been to be with you these past several days. I finally feel like I have my little boy back. I know you've been struggling, and we still may not be out of the woods yet, but I feel closer to you than I have in a long, long time. I feel like you've opened up and let me in again. Maybe something good has come out of this awful experience after all."

He looked at his mom and said, "Strange and mysterious ways, Mom. Maybe He's just working in strange and mysterious ways again."

Ding!!!!!!

This time Toby thought he could feel it coming together. As he lay there quietly, snippets of memory came to him slowly, fragments, a piece at a time. Vague, fuzzy pictures of a young boy named John Mark, his mother Mary, and other women, men named Peter and John. A place called Bethany and a man called Lazarus, a city named Jerusalem, an awful place called Golgotha, and a beautiful garden outside the city. And most especially, a man, a man named Jesus, Jesus of Nazareth.

Memories were funny, though. There were times Toby thought he remembered something, only later to discover that it was really just a photograph which must have gotten translated into a memory. There were also times when he would have a vivid dream, only later to believe that parts of the dream were actually memories. Then there were times when something actually did happen, but his memories of the event were only partial and fragmented, like it might have been a dream or may not have actually happened at all. As these memories began to emerge with more clarity Toby began to wonder if they might be real, but he quickly dismissed the thought. *That's preposterous,* he thought, *I was only out for three days, but those memories cover over three years. It had to be a dream when I was in the coma. None of it was real . . . Gosh, but it felt so real.* As he lay there in the darkness some new memories worked their way to the surface. The smell of freshly baked bread. Aromas wafting in on the breeze from the city during the Passover feast. The smell of ripe pomegranates in the little grove in the front courtyard. The smell of the large fig tree over his terrace. *Hey, wait a minute,* he thought, *how do you remember smells if they never happened? I've never even seen a fig! How can I know what a ripe one smells like on the tree?*

I know! he thought. *The mezuzah! I need to find the mezuzah!* He got up quietly and searched through all his things. Nothing. He went to the laundry area and searched through the clothes he had been wearing. Nothing. He looked under his bed and all over the floor of his room. Nothing. *Well, I guess that settles it,* he thought, dejectedly. *It was all just a dream.*

Sunday morning he awoke to an aroma he knew wasn't a dream—bacon frying! And eggs cooking! His favorite breakfast! He flew out of the bed and scampered down the hall, but stopped just short of the kitchen when he heard something. It was something beautiful, something sweet and beautiful that warmed his heart. His mom was singing, singing to herself as she cooked his breakfast. He couldn't remember the last time he had heard her sing. And it was beautiful. Hearing this made Toby feel happy. Really, honest-to-goodness happy. This was a feeling he hadn't felt in quite some time— since before his dad died, of course. And in that moment he realized something very important. He realized he could be happy even though his dad had been taken from him. He could miss his dad and love his dad, but still be happy. And so could his mom.

This thought triggered another memory fragment. Something about being reunited with his dad; about a mansion with many rooms, about a place where anyone who believes and has faith will go. *Faith!* thought Toby. *That's it—faith! I just have to have faith that I'll figure this out. I should just relax, and stop trying so hard, and maybe it will come to me. I just need to have faith.*

Images began to flood into his mind in rich, vivid relief. He recalled his conversation with Jesus atop the "thinking rock" when Jesus asked him if he would still believe the stars were in the sky, even if he couldn't see them. He remembered the faith of the centurion, the feeding of the five thousand, walking on water on the Sea of Galilee. Faith was the main factor in all these events. He remembered how Peter's faith at first failed him, but then saved him. He thought about all the healings, and how Jesus told each and every one that it was their faith that had made them whole. He remembered Jesus telling him to have faith that God was in control, even if Toby didn't understand some of the things He did. Most of all, he remembered hearing Jesus in the Garden of Gethsemane, when he pleaded with the Father to deliver him from his fate . . . and how resolute Jesus was once he determined it was the Father's will that he see it through.

These images were crystal clear, and it all led Toby to one inescapable conclusion: it didn't matter if these things were real or not—they were deeply meaningful and they were a part of him. Real or imagined, they were real to him. And more importantly, they must be there for a reason!

CHAPTER 27

Angels Among Us

"For they are like the angels.
They are God's children."

Luke 20:36

AFTER BREAKFAST TOBY AND HIS mom walked to church. This time, though, he didn't take a short-cut, because he was in no hurry, no hurry at all. In fact, he wished the time he was spending with his mom would last forever. His clothes didn't feel that uncomfortable today, and for some reason his good shoes didn't even seem to hurt as much. It was a beautiful day. The morning sun was shining, there was a gentle breeze blowing through the trees, and there wasn't a cloud in the sky. Toby felt really comfortable. So comfortable, in fact, that he didn't feel the need to talk. He was just enjoying the moment. His mom looked down at him just as he was looking up at her. She just smiled softly and took his hand in hers. Toby beamed. This was just about perfect. Toby's mom was excited because it wasn't often she got to attend Sunday School and church. She walked Toby into the building and as they separated to go to their Sunday School rooms she bent over and gave him a little kiss. Then she said, "How about if today you pass on the mission work after church and we'll just spend a relaxing afternoon together." Wow! Just when he thought things couldn't possibly get better, they did!

When he entered his Sunday School room everybody seemed happy to see him and pleased he wasn't hurt too badly. Everybody was so nice to him, which was kind of unusual. Toby didn't quite

188

know what to make of it. His teacher got everyone's attention and said, "Today marks a new chapter in our Bible study. If you'll recall, last week we finished up with Matthew, and today we begin the Gospel according to Mark."

Matthew, thought Toby. *For someone they all hated, what a nice man he turned out to be.* He caught himself thinking this and was a little shocked. *Where in the world did that come from?* he wondered.

The teacher went on to say, "Throughout the Gospel according to Mark we see the influence of Peter, but it is not likely that Peter wrote it . . ."

Ahhh, Peter, thought Toby, *the Rock!* and again he shuddered, bewildered by his own familiarity with Jesus' most trusted and dependable Disciple. *Dependable?* he found himself thinking. *How about denying even knowing Jesus, or sleeping when he was supposed to be on watch in the Garden.* Once again he had shocked himself.

His teacher said, "As best we can tell, it was written by a young man named Mark, who may have actually travelled with Peter as he preached. It is thought that Mark was the son of a lady named Mary who lived in Jerusalem. The upper room of her home was a meeting place for Jesus and the Disciples, and we think it was also the site of the Last Supper."

John Mark! thought Toby, *That's my John Mark!"* Toby's hand instinctively went to his chest searching for the mezuzah, but came back empty. *No doubt about it, that's my John Mark, though,* he thought, a full picture of John Mark forming in his mind's eye. He also began to remember in great detail many of the things he and John Mark did, and then it dawned on him—*Omigosh! He did it! He actually did it! He wrote down all his "stories," and a good many of them really did come from Peter, too.* Toby stopped in mid-recollection and thought, *Wait! How on earth do I know these things? This is starting to get a little scary!*

"When I was in divinity school," continued his teacher, "we played a game, a sort of mystery game, because some of the things in Mark's Gospel have no clear explanation. For example, we're told of an incident in which a man named Nicodemus came to Jesus under cover of darkness to ask him questions. Now, how is it that we know this?"

Toby raised his hand. "Toby," said his teacher, "I wasn't sure your arms could actually go up in the air—you've never raised your hand in here before. But since you have, and so politely at that, what is it you would like to contribute?"

"Well," said Toby, "suppose it's a first-hand account. Suppose John Mark followed Jesus and eavesdropped on the conversation."

"Hold on a minute," interrupted the teacher, "who is John Mark?" he said, eyeing Toby somewhat suspiciously.

Toby said, "I'm sorry, I meant Mark. I don't know where 'John Mark' came from. I meant Mark."

The teacher said, "And what about Jesus' statement to Judas at the Last Supper, 'What you are going to do, do quickly'? In that noisy, crowded room how could anyone have heard the exchange between Jesus and Judas?"

Again, Toby raised his hand. "Twice in a row," the teacher said, smiling, "Yes, Toby?"

"Same thing," said Toby, "Suppose John Mark—I mean Mark— and a friend of his were servers at the Last Supper, and when they were able to rest, one of them sat right behind Jesus and Judas. He would have been able to hear what nobody else in the room could hear."

"The Garden of Gethsemane, too, Toby?" asked the teacher. "Jesus was alone in the Garden and the three Disciples were asleep. How do we know what Jesus said? The 'eavesdropper' again, I suppose?"

"Hey, coulda happened," said Toby, nodding knowingly. Then he added almost absent-mindedly, "It's thick with scrub, and plenty of places to hide. And right at the opening there's this little thicket, with just enough room to squeeze in there and listen. The big cypress trees block out a lot of the wind, so it's pretty quiet, too. If you hold your breath you can hear lots of things."

The room fell silent, all eyes on Toby. He looked up and saw everyone looking at him. He panicked, but quickly recovered: "Hey, Google Earth," he said, shrugging his shoulders. "I looked it up on Google Earth, what can I say?" he said.

"Of course," said his teacher, "Of course," and the room relaxed once again.

"You know," said his teacher, "Toby's theory could actually be our answer. In Mark's Gospel, and only in Mark's Gospel, we're told there was a young boy who was discovered with Jesus and the others when the mob showed up to arrest Jesus. In fact, the soldiers tried to nab him but instead of grabbing the boy, they just got hold of his tunic. The tunic came off, and the boy ran away naked."

The other boys and girls started to giggle. Normally Toby would have been a ringleader in the giggling, but instead he said, "Hey, it's not funny! How would you like to run through scrub and brambles completely naked and have to sneak back into the upper room . . . with a big, ugly, angry Roman legionnaire after you?"

Again, the room fell quiet and Toby felt everyone's eyes on him once again. He wasn't sure whether they were shocked by the intensity of what he said or simply because instead of giggling he was showing empathy for the boy, so he said, "I mean, how would you feel? Besides, Jesus had just been arrested and the boy was probably really scared, you know?" As he had hoped, they were struck by his empathy for the boy.

His teacher said, "Wow, Toby, I'm impressed by what you've been able to read into this story, looking below the surface and seeing things in context."

"Well," said Toby, "I guess it's something I've thought a lot about . . . since the coma, you know?"

Then his teacher said, "Speaking of young boys in the Gospel of Mark, there's one more incident involving a young boy which only occurs in Mark's Gospel. Does anyone know what it is?" All the children looked around at each other, at a loss.

Finally, Toby said, "Well, I think there might have been a young boy in the empty tomb after Jesus was resurrected . . . and he startled Mary of Magdala, Mary the mother of John, and Salome when they came to finish anointing Jesus' body. He told the women that they wouldn't find Jesus there, that he had been resurrected. And he told them to go remind Peter and the Disciples that Jesus said he would meet them in Galilee."

"It was probably an angel," said one boy. "Or Jesus," said another, "and they just thought he looked like a boy!" A little girl piped up and said, "Who said it had to be a little boy—it could have been a girl with short hair and they mistook her for a boy!" Then the other children joined in a lively discussion about just who the figure in white might have been.

Now, by this time Toby knew to be careful, and to not just blurt out the truth of the matter. He simply said, "You know, the writer of the Gospel, Mark, said it was a boy . . . maybe we ought to just take his word for it that it was a boy . . . maybe even Mark himself . . . or even a friend of Mark's who came back and told him about it," he said.

"Well now, let's not get too far-fetched here," said the teacher, "but I'm glad to see that everyone is thinking. Between now and next week why don't you guys give some thought to these issues. Tell me what you think of Toby's 'first person' theory, or see if you can come up with a better one. And Toby, again, welcome back. It's been a pleasure having you in my class today." Despite the "too far-fetched" comment, Toby found himself beaming.

After church Toby passed on the mission work and walked home with his mom. His head was spinning from the memories that had been flowing back to him. He was struck by the fact that these memories seemed as real as if the events had happened just yesterday.

His mom fixed them a nice lunch, and as they ate they discussed their Sunday School lessons and the pastor's sermon, but Toby left out the "Google Earth" thing.

His mom told him about the pastor's sermon, which was called "We're All God's Angels." When Toby heard the title he couldn't help but giggle, thinking, *At least we're better looking than the one that I saw.* And then he thought, *The one I saw. Did I really say that? Geez . . . Did I really see him? I couldn't have just made that up. If I had made it up he would have been handsome and dashing like all the pictures of angels I've ever seen . . .* He giggled again as he thought, *Well, at least it explains why the very first words out of their mouths are always "Fear not."*

She continued, "In his sermon the pastor talked about the importance of always trying to do God's will, to be kind to others, to think of them before ourselves, to be merciful and forgiving, and to try to be holy, just as He is holy. He said, 'Just a simple act of kindness, a little act of selflessness, a thoughtful comment or act, you never know the kind of impact such a thing might have on someone else. Someone who, in that particular moment, may have desperately needed a kind word, a gentle touch, or just some measure of human kindness to get them out of a funk, to let them know that at least someone cares, or to help get them through their day. When we act as the Father would have us act, we never know the power of our actions. That's why we have to try and do His will at all times, because we never know which little act may have a lifelong impact on someone else. For in those small moments we're God's angels, His ambassadors, His helpers. In those moments, His will is being done right here on earth, just as it is in heaven.'"

His helpers, thought Toby. *So it's more than just a one-time thing. It's really about how you live your life day-to-day. I can still be a helper, even though I'm not there anymore. But wait a minute!* he thought. *Not where anymore?*

As these thoughts ran through his head his mom just talked and talked, more animated and happier than he had seen her in a long, long time. But Toby must have had "that look" on his face, because his mom suddenly stopped talking and looked at him with incredible sympathy and compassion. She said, "Toby, I'm so sorry. I've just been going on and on in my excitement without a thought about how tired you must be. I'm afraid I've worn you out with my yapping," she said. "Instead of listening to me go on and on you should be resting. Let's get you back to your room and in bed."

Toby didn't know what to say, so he just nodded. His mom walked him back to his room, and as he was laying down on his bed she suddenly said, "Oh, I meant to tell you. I found something when I went to wash the clothes you were wearing the day you got hurt." She left the room and returned a few moments later holding something in her hand. "I don't know what this is," she said, looking down at it, "but it's very nice, like a trinket or something you might wear around your neck."

Toby sat bolt upright in the bed, his eyes wide and his fatigue completely forgotten. "Where did you find it?" he asked.

"They said that you were clutching this in your hand when they found you," she said, "and the strand was broken, for some reason. They gave it to me at the hospital when they gave me your things. I didn't think about it until I went to wash your clothes, and it was wrapped up in them. I thought perhaps it was a mistake and might have belonged to someone else, since I had never seen it before. I put it in my jewelry box for safe keeping, and I just now remembered it."

"No, no! It's not a mistake!" exclaimed Toby. He was excited, but bewildered as well. She handed it to him and he clutched it tightly, holding it to his chest, and before he knew it tears were falling on it. "It really is mine," he said quietly. "It was given to me by a friend. It's called a mezuzah, and it has a prayer inside."

"A friend," she said. "Which one?" Actually, she didn't think that Toby had many friends and was rather surprised.

"A boy named John Mark," he said.

"I guess I don't know him," she said. "What kind of prayer is inside?"

Toby showed her how to open it, and she took the piece of parchment out and looked at it. "Toby, I can't read this," she said. "It's in a foreign language, I think. It looks like maybe it's written in Hebrew!"

Toby laughed and said, "Oh yeah. It is, mom. John Mark is Jewish."

"Well, do you know what the prayer says?" she asked, bewildered.

"Of course," said Toby. "It's from the book of Deuteronomy, and it says 'Hear, O Israel: the Lord our God, the Lord is One.' And the writing on the parchment is from a real Temple scribe, too."

"What do you mean, from a real Temple scribe?" she asked.

Toby stammered, thinking fast. "Er…. uh…. I think he said that one of the scribes at his temple actually wrote the prayer for him. His dad was killed in an accident, too, and he gave me this so I could not only think about God and have Him close to my heart, but also about dad."

"That's very nice," said his mom, "very touching. He must be a very good friend. I'd like to meet him sometime. If he thinks this much of you, he must have seen something in you. He must have seen the real you. I'm sure I'd like him very much."

All of a sudden Toby saw everything with great clarity. He finally understood his role as Jesus' helper. Toby had been witness to some of the greatest events in human history! He was there when John the Baptist baptized Jesus and the heavens opened. He witnessed the wilderness ordeal when Satan tempted Jesus. He carried the basket that contained the loaves and fishes. Because of John Mark's illness, Toby saw Satan enter into Judas at Simon the Leper's home. He heard the money bag jingle with thirty pieces of silver when the Temple Priests paid off the traitor Judas. Without him, no one would know what Jesus whispered to Judas at the Last Supper. No one would know about Jesus' pleading with the father to "let the cup pass" as he prayed in the Garden. And no one would know what really happened that morning of the resurrection. The stories that John Mark wrote down became known as "The Gospel of Mark," one of the holiest books in the entire Bible. And many of the stories came from Toby himself, telling John Mark what he had witnessed.

So that's what being a helper was all about! thought Toby. *Jesus was right. You have no idea how much of a help you're being, even when doing the simplest of things.* Everything came together—the memories, the smells, the fear, the worry, and the joy. Especially the joy. The joy that comes from forgiving others. The joy that comes from cleansing your heart of bad feelings. The joy that comes from menial service to others. The joy that comes from keeping your eyes on the prize and trying to do God's will on earth as it is in Heaven. In short, the joy that comes from a personal relationship with Jesus, the Christ. It all came together for him.

Toby sat up in his bed suddenly and said, "Mom, there's something I have to do," as he rushed to his closet, saying, "but I have to change my clothes first."

"Where on earth do you think you're going?" she asked. "You need to rest."

"I will, mom, I will . . . as soon as I get back from Ms. Yancey's house—there's some work I need to do there . . . I think maybe she's someone who could use a helper."

Amen.

CPSIA information can be obtained
at www.ICGtesting.com
Printed in the USA
FSHW01n2114170818
51545FS